Look Through
My Window

Look Through My Window

by

Jean Little

HarperCollins*Publishers*Ltd

First published in the U.S. by HarperCollins Publishers: 1970
First HarperCollins Publishers Ltd Canadian edition: 1995

Canadian Cataloguing in Publication Data

Little, Jean, 1932-
   Look through my window

1st HarperCollins Canadian ed.
ISBN 0-00-648078-0

I. Title.

PS8523.I77L66 1995   jC813'.54   C95-931702-3
PZ7.L57Lo 1995

---

95 96 97 98 99 ❖ OPM 10 9 8 7 6 5 4 3 2 1

Printed and bound in the United States

for Chris
     Brian,
     Adam,
     Martin
     Robin
     Maggie
     Allison,
     Peter,
     Kyrie,
     Mark,
     and Sarah
with my love

Contents

1

The Day the World Changed

T he door would not open.

Emily Blair did not believe it. She gave the knob an extra twist and pushed harder. Nothing happened. Apartment 14A stayed locked against her.

The girl stood and searched her memory for an explanation. Her mother must have said that morning that she was going to the hairdresser or the dentist. But Mother had not mentioned an appointment.

Even when her daughter had dashed back for the math book she had left on her desk, Elizabeth

Blair had only called after her the usual "Have a good day, dear."

All at once Emily saw herself standing there, brought to a halt by a closed door. After all, she *did* know what to do! She was not helpless without her mother, whatever Mother might think. She reached in the milk box, felt for the extra door key, and used it.

"Mother," she called.

She knew there would be no answer. The rooms opening out of the hall echoed with emptiness. Emily, moving to shut the door behind her, tiptoed, and she jumped when it latched with a sharp click.

"You're crazy!" she muttered to herself.

But she shivered suddenly, even as she spoke, for it was strange. Always before, Mrs. Blair had been there waiting, after school, or, if she had to be out, she made arrangements for her daughter to go home with one of the other girls. Emily could not remember ever being alone in the apartment with no idea where her mother was, until now.

"It's sort of interesting, really," she said out loud. Her voice boomed in the silence. Quickly, she began to hunt for clues.

A cup of coffee sat on one corner of the dining table. Mother must have made it and left it to cool a little. Emily touched the rim of the cup. The coffee was cold.

Moments later, she found her mother's lunch dishes by the kitchen sink. This time, Emily's surprise came close to alarm. Elizabeth Blair never failed to rinse, stack, wash, and dry dishes as soon as a meal was over. Not only had she left these dishes unwashed—they had not been rinsed, and they had been shoved together in an untidy jumble.

Something frightening, something urgent, must have happened. Mother was not acting like herself.

Emily turned to go for help—and saw the note taped to the refrigerator door.

Relief washed over her as she reached for it, but she sighed too. She should have known she would find an ordinary, everyday, sensible explanation waiting for her somewhere. If she were a girl in a TV show, it might yet turn out to be a demand for ransom. But no cold finger of real fear touched her in the instant before she began to read. It would be from Mother and it would make all the strangeness, all the excitement, vanish. It would be a neat, practical note, explaining everything.

But was it from her mother? Emily took it nearer the window where she could see better.

Emily,

I don't know when I'll be back. If your father gets there first, tell him I had to go to Roger's. Only he won't because he had an appointment with Mr. Gresham. The supper is in the oven and it will turn itself on.

It pays to freeze things! I must go! I'll explain later. Don't worry about anything.

Mother

Not even "Love, Mother," the girl noted.

Trying to make sense out of it, she read the message through again. The whole thing sounded wrong. Mother always took time to explain. Often she explained things Emily already understood perfectly. Not only that, but she always knew when she would be back from anywhere.

Something drastic must have happened at Uncle Roger's.

Emily did not waste time trying to imagine what. Her four small cousins—John, James, Jean, and Ann Sutherland—were always doing drastic things. James had set the house on fire once. John had driven the family car, slowly, into a nearby telephone pole. A month ago, Ann had swallowed the top off a toothpaste tube. And Jean, the dreamy one, got lost regularly.

To Emily they were like children in a story. She did not see them often, even though Uncle Roger was Mother's only brother. The Blairs' apartment was too small to hold the six Sutherlands overnight. If her cousins had been closer to her in age, Emily might have gone sometimes to stay at the farmhouse where they lived, but John, the oldest, was just seven. Once in a while, she and her parents did drive out and spend a

Sunday afternoon there, but more often they talked of going, only to decide against it. Uncle Roger's job as a salesman kept him away from his wife and children so much of the time.

"If he's away, Deborah doesn't need extra people on her hands," Emily's mother would say, "and if he's home, they deserve to have themselves to themselves."

The girl alone in Apartment 14A looked uneasily at the note she now knew by heart. The more she thought about it, the stranger it became. Had Mother ever gone flying off to the Sutherlands' like this before? No. Not even that time James had shot his father in the leg with his friend's new BB gun! Aunt Deborah had just written one of her funny letters after it was all over . . .

Remembering, Emily was back for a moment in that evening months before. Her parents must have thought she was already asleep or they would have kept their voices down. Right in the middle of reading Aunt Deborah's letter aloud, Mother had interrupted herself.

"Peter, do you ever wonder if there's something the matter with Emily?" she asked.

Emily was so startled she almost let out a telltale yelp. Instead, she lay still, straining both ears.

"One or another of Roger's children is always in trouble, but Emily has always been . . . sensible and calm. Sometimes I wonder if she's almost *too* good . . ."

"I've done bad things," the girl in the next

room muttered under her breath. She was not at all pleased with this picture of herself.

Dad laughed.

"Worry no longer," he said, still laughing. "Emily's not that close to perfection yet. She has several endearing vices."

"Well, I know it's silly," Mother admitted, but then Dad spoke again, more slowly.

"Come to think of it, though, she never seems to get terribly excited about anything . . ."

"I do so," his daughter protested in a whisper. But she could not remember when.

"Now *you're* being silly," Mother said. "Listen to the rest of this about James . . ."

As she read on, there was horror in her voice, but Emily, unable to sleep now, heard admiration there too.

Coming back to the present, she wondered what on earth James had done this time.

Then, in the space of a breath, she forgot him. Her mother's note dropped unheeded to the counter top. She stood stock-still, finally taking in the magnificent truth.

She, Emily Ann Blair, was alone. Utterly, entirely alone! And she was going to go on being alone for at least two hours.

Nobody was here to tell her to clean up the clutter in her room or start her homework or set the table for supper. She did not even have to go swimming in the pool downstairs, as she herself had planned. Why, she could do nothing! If she chose, she could just sit and stare into space—for two hours! Nobody would even offer her a penny for her thoughts.

Suddenly, irrepressibly, she spun around in the middle of the kitchen floor.

Now . . . what next?

The phone shrilled a summons.

As Emily ran to answer it, her aloneness grew real again. She reached for the receiver, not looking behind her into the shadowy bedrooms.

Not that fat Sharon, she wished in the instant before she said hello. Not Ruth. Not even Moira. Let it be for Mother.

Her magic powers failed.

"Emily, you want me to come by for you?" Ruth said in her whiney voice.

Emily, knowing Ruth was safely in C Block, made a rude face at her through the phone.

The two of them were not special friends. Ruth was simply one of the horde of children who lived in the Court. They came and went as their parents changed jobs, but there was always a gang of them left. On hot afternoons like this, they collected at the pool. On cold or rainy days, they met in front of somebody's television set.

They were an accepted part of Emily's days, like school, like getting up in the morning. Ruth and Sharon were the same age as she was and Moira was a year older. Moira made it clear that she only put up with the other three because there were no girls her age in the apartments.

"I'm not coming," Emily told Ruth.

"What do you mean, you're not coming?"

Emily understood the other girl's surprise. Sometimes Ruth came to get Emily. Sometimes Emily went to pick up Moira or Ruth—or even Sharon. But always, on an afternoon like this, they all ended up at the pool—unless, of course, a mother interfered.

Emily opened her mouth to say she had to stay in and help her mother. But suddenly she was tired of Ruth, tired of her babyish voice when she did not get her own way, tired of her long black hair which reached all the way to her waist—a good four inches longer than Emily's.

"I'm just not coming," she said. "I don't feel like it. So there's no use coming to get me."

"Don't FEEL like it!" Ruth repeated, amazed.

Emily held the receiver away from her ear and smiled.

I don't even have to give her a good reason, she thought.

"Ruth, shut up and listen to me," she cut in on the other girl. "Try to understand this. I just do not want to go!"

"What DO you want to do?" asked Ruth, all agog.

She was prepared for something really startling, Emily could tell. She herself was silent, looking for an answer.

"Emily, I said—" Ruth began.

"I heard you," Emily retorted, her joy ebbing. Then she remembered. "I want to do nothing," she said. "It's my own business anyway, what I do. I'll see you tomorrow."

She hung up although she could hear Ruth saying something more. For a moment she stood waiting, almost wishing Ruth would call her back. Even after she knew the phone was not going to ring, she did not move. How did one do nothing? Where?

The heat, pressing down on her like warm syrup, decided it. Walking slowly and carefully, as if she were in a dream, Emily went into her bedroom and, still in her school clothes, stretched out full-length on her bed. She lay there, not stirring, for almost an hour. She did not even think about anything in particular. She was doing nothing with every inch of herself. Deep within her, she experienced a quiet contentment in knowing that, for a while, no bell would ring, no teacher would ask a question, no child would call for her, no parent would want her to begin or finish anything.

Before she was interrupted, she herself tired of it. She got up and changed her creased dress for cool shorts and a sleeveless shirt. She scooped her mane of dark-brown hair into twin ponytails. Then she wrote a poem.

The first two verses were easy; they came out of her conversation with Ruth, out of her surprise at finding the apartment empty. The rest was work. She perched on the edge of her bed, writing out bits, erasing them smudgily, putting

in something different. At last she thought she
had it. Skipping the many scribbled-out lines,
she read it through.

> When I wake up,
> I always know
> What I'll do
> And where I'll go,
>
> Whom I'll see
> And what we'll say
> And who I'll be
> The whole long day.
>
> If ever I
> Did something new,
> They all would say,
> "That's not like you."
>
> I'm always just
> The me they see—
> Not the real true
> Inside me.
>
> But now they're gone.
> I'm free, free, FREE !
> I'll be the real true
> Emily.

Yes. That was it exactly. As always when she
had first finished one of her poems, Emily

wanted to sing, to dance, to shout. Instead she read her own words over and over till she knew every syllable by heart.

Then she wanted to share them with someone. Who? Thrusting the poem from her, she jumped up and prowled restlessly through the apartment. She flipped the television on—and off. She picked up a magazine—and dropped it. She was so hot! She blew up at her bangs, but they clung limply to her forehead. A glass of lemonade! That was what she needed.

But the poem followed her everywhere. Who was this "real true Emily"? Was there such a person?

Emily drank deeply of the lemonade, wishing she had never written the words and, yet, still stubbornly pleased with them. Maybe if she changed the last verse somehow . . . She started to go and get it, changed her mind, and slumped into a chair.

The apartment door opened. Dizzy with relief, she scrambled up and ran to meet her father.

"I thought you were going to be late!" she cried.

Just in time, she remembered she was not a child. Instead of flinging her arms around him, she drew back. He studied her, startled first by her eager welcome and then by her withdrawal.

"It's after seven," he said. "Where's your mother?"

Emily was in the middle of an explanation when the door opened again. Elizabeth Blair had come home.

"What happened to you?" Dad started.

But Mother did not need to be asked. She sank down on the couch, kicked off her shoes, and began to talk.

"Oh, Peter," she plunged in, "wait until I tell you! Deborah has tuberculosis."

The truth of what she was saying seemed to shock her anew as she spoke the words aloud, but she hesitated only long enough to take a deep breath.

"She and Roger went to one of those mobile chest X-ray clinics at the school. Neither of them thought a thing about it till yesterday when their doctor called. He asked her to come in and suggested Roger come too. They even joked about it after he phoned!"

"TB," Dad said, as though he had not heard anything after Mother named the illness.

"The doctor told her she'll be fine—but it will take time. Maybe as long as a year! A year, Peter!"

"Okay, I know. It's rough." Dad sat down heavily on the couch beside her and reached for her hand.

"Thank goodness Roger was home for a change! She's to go into the hospital next week."

"How does Aunt Deborah look?" Emily asked.

Instantly she wished she had kept quiet, but her mother answered as though she had wondered at it herself.

"She looks fine. A bit thin, but Deb's always

thin. She keeps saying she doesn't feel sick at all. Just a bit tired. They're getting a Red Cross Homemaker to help out till she goes, but after that . . . Roger said he'd find a housekeeper, but I told him he couldn't possibly. Not with four children and their house being in the country!"

"Well, what *is* he going to do?" Peter Blair asked.

Abruptly there was silence. Mother looked at Dad, at Emily, at the floor. For no sensible reason Emily had a feeling that the three of them were, all of a sudden, standing together on the edge of a cliff.

"Elizabeth . . ." Dad prodded gently.

"I said . . . I said WE would take the children," Mother blurted.

"I don't know what came over me." She rushed on before Emily or her father could do more than gasp. "I know, I know. It's utterly impossible. But I thought maybe we could rent a cottage . . . for the summer at least. I don't think I could handle life on that farm—and there isn't really enough room there. They're crowded now. Roger was so desperate, Peter, and Deb . . . Deb cried. I've never seen her in tears before, not in all the years we've known each other. I wanted to call you, but I couldn't get through. PETER! Your interview! I forgot all about it! What did he want?"

"We're being transferred," Emily's father said quietly.

Emily, seeing his lips twitch, was astounded. Yet, it *was* funny the way everything was piling up so fast. Funny—and frightening. She sat down carefully on the nearest chair and went on listening. Even if later none of this turned out to be real, she did not want to miss a word.

"I've been made manager of the Royal Bank of Canada in Riverside, Ontario, population forty-five thousand. Are you impressed?"

"Oh, Peter," Mother said faintly.

He patted her hand and went on explaining, giving her time to recover.

"George Appleton had a coronary, and they've nobody to take his place. I'm to go there immediately myself, and we'll all move as soon as possible. Mr. Gresham was apologetic about giving such short notice, but things are already in a muddle there."

"Transferred," Elizabeth Blair told herself.

"I'm afraid the cottage idea is out, Elizabeth. And you'd never survive on the farm with five children, especially those kids of Roger's."

"I'm terrified of them," Mother admitted. "What on earth are we going to do?"

"I'll go to Riverside tomorrow and start looking for a house we can rent," Dad answered. "I'll get a place big enough for the lot of us—and we can all move."

"Move . . . all of us!"

Mother sounded out of breath. Emily understood. She felt breathless herself.

"Why not?" retorted Peter Blair.

His daughter blinked. All her life, he had cautioned her to think ahead, plan carefully, weigh the cost of whatever she wanted to do. "Look before you leap" he often said. Mother even called him "Look-Before-You-Leap-Blair" sometimes, although she herself was a planner. Emily stared first at one, then at the other. Were they serious?

"Peter, Peter!" Mother wailed, settling Emily's doubts. "The whole thing is impossible."

"We'll work it out somehow," Dad said.

"Maybe we were in a rut, Elizabeth," he went on, feeling his way among unfamiliar thoughts. "When I was a boy in Riverside, I dreamed of owning a house there—but I haven't thought of it in years. I . . . we're still young."

He broke off abruptly.

"Elizabeth," he said, "look at Emily."

Mrs. Blair, without a word, turned to study her daughter.

Emily's blue eyes mirrored the shock in her mother's. In a matter of minutes, without any warning, their world had changed. The first lines of her poem jingled suddenly in her head.

When I wake up,
I always know
What I'll do
And where I'll go . . .

That had been true of all three of them that very morning. Now not one of them had any idea what waited in tomorrow. It would be new though. It would be an adventure.

And, she thought, with a sweep of ridiculous joy, it will happen to the real true Emily. I know it!

It was sad about Aunt Deborah. She knew that too. She even knew that she, Emily, would be frightened sometimes, moving to a strange place. But neither of these things seemed important right now.

She leaped up, unable to sit still a moment longer. Then while her mother stared and her father smiled, Emily Blair did a jig, a sudden silly jubilant dance all her own. She could hardly wait!

2

The House, the Room, and the Box

"I needn't warn a banker not to do anything rash," Elizabeth Blair teased her husband as he left for Riverside the next morning.

"Look before you leap," Emily advised, taking her turn at it.

"I've told you today will be mostly business," Peter Blair reminded them. "I'll try to find out what houses are available, but that's all I'll have time for."

He did not arrive home till Emily was halfway through her homework. He stood in the doorway, looking from his wife to his daughter as though they were both people he was seeing for the first time.

"Peter, what is it?" Mother asked, getting up and going to him.

"I bought a house," he said. "I've made the down payment already."

"You bought . . ."

Words failed his wife. Now it was she who stared as though he had grown two heads or turned green since breakfast.

"It has eighteen rooms," Dad said firmly.

He doesn't believe it either, Emily thought.

"Peter, you're joking. Surely you're joking."

"No. Eighteen. I counted them. I'll take you to see it tomorrow."

"Can I go?" Emily begged. "Please!"

"Of course not. You have to go to school," her mother snapped. She shot Emily an angry look—and then looked bewildered by her own bad temper. Not apologizing, she turned back to her husband.

"I'm telling you the truth, Elizabeth," he assured her before she could ask him again. "I can't explain. I just had to have it. When I was a boy, it was a beautiful place. We used to watch the people through the windows sometimes, having parties . . . To see it like that!"

"Like what?" Elizabeth Blair barely managed to keep from shrieking.

"Didn't I tell you?" her husband said, still

looking back to his boyhood. "It hasn't been lived in for eleven years."

"Oh, Peter," moaned Mother, "what have you done?"

The last days of school always crawled by, but for Emily Blair this year they hardly seemed to move at all. She kept trying to picture a house with eighteen rooms, a house that had been left empty for such a long time. When the teacher asked her a question, Emily blushed, swallowed, and admitted she had not been listening.

The teacher sighed. For her too the time went slowly.

Then, the last bell rang. It was over. Only a matter of hours . . .

When the car climbed the hill and pulled to a halt in front of the house, Emily sat and said not a word. None of the hundreds of houses she had imagined measured up to this. It was enormous. It looked big enough for four or five families. It was bulky and white with dark green shutters. A deep shadowy verandah ran across the front and down one side.

But it was not only the size of the house that held Emily speechless. It seemed to her to be adrift in the middle of a sea of growth. What looked, to the apartment child, like miles of uncut grass billowed in green waves around it. Vines clambered up the posts of the verandah. And there were trees everywhere. Big as the house was, two giant evergreens overtopped it in front.

"Emily Ann Blair, are you going to spend the whole day sitting with your mouth hanging open?" Mother demanded.

Emily shut her mouth and sprang out of the car.

"Is this really ours?" she breathed.

"Don't look at me," her mother said. "I refuse to assume any responsibility for this whatsoever."

"Come and see," Dad invited, ignoring his wife.

They reached the verandah. Even Emily could see that it badly needed painting. She walked softly. Still, she could hear her footsteps echo in the empty rooms inside.

"It sounds haunted," she half-whispered.

"Haunted by mice and spiders," Mother told her.

"Your cousins will soon drive out any ghosts," Dad said.

A moment later, the three of them stood together in the front hall.

"What does it remind you of?" Emily asked. She herself thought it like a cave.

"Westminster Abbey," Mother said. "Emily, we have things to measure and so on. Do you want to stay with us or go exploring on your own?"

"Exploring," Emily said bravely.

Then, all at once, the house felt friendly after all. She sped away from the adults, up the stairs.

She would investigate the ground floor later. Now she wanted to find her own place in this incredible, wonderful house which was actually going to be home.

The stairs turned and divided at the landing. Opening doors, Emily found six bedrooms and two bathrooms. Four of the bedrooms had open fireplaces in them just like the bedrooms in Misselthwaite Manor. Emily, who dearly loved *The Secret Garden*, thought of choosing one of these rooms for hers. But she pressed on. There were two more closed doors. The first led, disappointingly, into a huge black closet. Emily backed out hastily, thinking of bats.

She opened the last door. She was at the foot of another flight of stairs. She hesitated for a split second. These stairs were narrow, uncarpeted, and uninviting. She listened. Far away, she could hear her mother laughing.

Concentrating on the dim light at the top, Emily started up.

Another hall and five more closed doors!

Emily began with the one closest to herself and worked her way around. They were strange rooms. The windows came in unexpected places, above your head or at your knees. The ceilings all sloped. There were three bedrooms, and another bathroom with a gigantic old-fashioned bathtub standing on claw feet in one corner of it.

One more door to go. She opened it very gently,

hoping against hope. Then she stood and just looked, her eyes shining.

It was a small room, made even smaller by the slant of the roof. At one side, the ceiling was only about three feet from the floor. It was the first room that was not wholly empty. In the far corner there was a jumble of boxes and a couple of cushions. Emily did not stop to investigate yet. She was gazing at the windows. Set into the slope of the roof was an actual skylight. It did not open. It was just a pane of frosted glass, but the light fell into the little room in a different way through it, almost as though the room itself were part of the sky, part of sun and rain and wind and cloud. The skylight made the room like Heidi's loft and Sara Crewe's garret.

If Ruth could only see it, Emily thought.

Then she knew, suddenly and positively, that she did not want Ruth to see it, not Ruth or Sharon or Moira or any of them. They would think it a pokey little room. They would not have read the right books. They would not understand.

There was another window, in the wall directly across from the door. Like the windows in the other attic rooms it was high in the wall, well above Emily's head. But it was a casement window, a round one, like a porthole, which swung outward.

If she just had something to climb on.

She hurried over to the corner. There were a couple of orange crates. Old bits of blanket had been spread on top of them to make them into seats. Cushions were propped up.

"Somebody's been here," Emily said right out loud.

Then she saw the little box. It was like a miniature cedar chest. Emily snatched it up. A sign had been pasted onto the top of it.

PRIVATE PROPERTY!!! KEEP OUT!!!
BY ORDER OF LINDSAY JANE ROSS

Then in smaller handwriting but blacker, sharper letters, it said:

> O, Intruder,
> Beware of the Beast!
>   Kate

"The nerve!" Emily said.

Her voice was shaking with excitement. Paying no attention to Lindsay Jane Ross's instructions or to Kate's warning, she pried at the catch. The box was locked.

"Rats!" Emily muttered. "I'll have to—"

"Are you up there, Emily?"

They were at the foot of the stairs.

"Yes," Emily called back.

Moving like lightning, she shoved cushions, blankets, and the mysterious box out of sight, into the depths of a closet, while her mother and father climbed the stairs to find her.

3

John, James, Jean, and Ann

Elizabeth Blair was not enchanted with the attic.

"What on earth will we put into all this space?" she asked, frowning at the streaked walls, the dusty, cobwebbed windows.

"Me," said Emily.

Neither of them understood at first. Until she saw refusal in their eyes, Emily had not known how badly she wanted the small, odd room she had discovered. Suddenly, terribly, she wanted it. She had to have it! Her parents hesitated, taken aback by the urgency in her face. Words tumbled out of her.

"I won't be in your way up here," she promised.

"But, Emily, you never have been in our way," her mother said.

"Maybe we've been in *her* way sometimes." Dad had hit on a truth Emily herself had barely glimpsed. "In all her life Emily's never been farther from us than the other side of a wall. And poets are supposed to live in garrets, Elizabeth."

He had seen it too, Emily thought. The little room under the eaves was made for writing poems in. If only her mother would understand!

"I suppose we could put John and James up here with you—if it matters that much," Mrs. Blair mused, watching her daughter.

Emily, about to turn away so that the surge of hope she felt would not show, realized, all at once, that she must share it. She faced them. "It does matter," she said, her heart in her voice.

"That's settled then," said her father. Her mother, speaking at the same time, said, "All right, Emily."

They were the ones who turned away, abashed by the blaze of delight on her face.

"Let's put a Ping-Pong table in this big room," Peter Blair said. "I've always wanted space enough for one."

"You're more of a child than she is," his wife answered, going to look.

Emily slipped away from them.

"You're mine," she told the room, "my very

own. No matter what that Kate thinks," she added.

Upending one of the orange crates, she climbed on it to her casement window. She struggled to open it. A cloud of dust made her sneeze and the window would not budge, but she kept at it, tugging and banging at the catch. Finally, it creaked open and she swung the window wide. Crossing her arms on the ledge, she rested her chin on them. Far below, she could see their own tangled garden and the neat lawns of their neighbors. She could even look down into the tops of trees. She felt like a bird.

She jumped down as her parents reached her doorway.

"Do you realize," her mother was saying in a tone of doom, "that those children will be here in THREE days? Three days—to move mountains."

Joy exploded inside Emily like a burst of band music. She dashed across the room and gave her mother a flying hug.

"Oh, Mother, isn't it exciting!" she gasped.

Elizabeth Blair looked down in wonder at the bright face raised to hers.

"Oh, Emily," she groaned. Then she relented.

"I suppose it is . . . different," she said, her voice softening. "But whenever the two of you feel ready to come back down to earth, we have work to do. Beginning now," she added firmly as Emily drew back.

The box, Emily thought. I have to look at that box!

"You go ahead," she suggested to her mother, trying to sound as though it did not matter to her one way or the other. "I'll be down in just a few minutes."

"No, you don't," Mother said. "I know you and your 'few minutes.' From now on, you are part of a team, and we stick together. You, Emily Ann, are my right-hand girl."

There was no escape. Mother shepherded Emily ahead of her down the stairs.

I'll be back the first chance I get, Emily silently promised the box hidden in her closet.

But when Elizabeth Blair said work, she meant it. For the next three days, Emily washed windows, chopped down long grass with unwieldy hand clippers, scrubbed layers on layers of dirt off woodwork, washed the verandah floor and the steps. By the second day, she had blisters on both hands. Her arms ached. Her fingernails were broken. Her knuckles stayed grimy even when she used a nail brush on them. She was actually beginning to wonder whether she did like this house after all.

Then she would remember her new room. Mother had come with her to clean it, so she had not been able to get at whatever Lindsay Jane Ross and the mysterious Kate had locked away. But the room had become more magical as the dirt disappeared.

"I suppose we'd better attack the closet while we're at it." Mother sighed, flexing her right arm to take some of the weariness out of it.

"Dad's calling you," Emily invented hurriedly. "I'm almost sure I hear him."

Elizabeth Blair left the room, went to the head of the stairs, finally went halfway down, listening for her husband's voice. Emily dove into the closet, grabbed up the box, looked frantically around the bare room, shot out into the hall and, in a flash of inspiration, darted into the bathroom and stuffed the box in behind the gargantuan bathtub.

"He wasn't calling," Mother said. "You're beginning to hear things, Emily."

She dragged the cushions and blankets out of the closet, but they were old and battered. Emily held her breath.

"I wonder how these got here," Mother said. She fingered one of the cushions, covered with dust from the floor. "Put them in that carton of junk in the hall, Emily."

"But—" Emily started to object.

"But what?" her mother asked.

"Nothing," Emily said and put Lindsay's and Kate's things into the garbage box.

I can get them new cushions, she thought.

She remembered then that she did not know them. She might never even meet them. Emily shook her head at that thought. Already she was certain that these girls were going to arrive any day, wanting their box back.

"But not till after I find out what's in it," she vowed, going back to washing woodwork.

On moving day it rained. Even Emily, who woke up feeling as though it were her birthday, was disheartened by the grey downpour. Still, it had come—the day she had been waiting for. That very night she would actually sleep in her new room. She sang as they left the apartment for the last time and dashed to the waiting car. The furniture van arrived an hour after they did. Emily's bed went directly under the casement window. Her long, low bookshelves fitted in against the wall under the slant of the roof. Her desk and chair were set where the light streamed in on them through the skylight. The room was still unpainted, but it was as clean as soap and water could get it.

"I'll have yellow walls," Emily told herself softly, standing and looking around her private kingdom, "and the woodwork will be white—"

"Emily!" her mother called from far below. "They're here!"

The children! Emily turned and raced down the stairs.

There they were with their father, just inside the front door. They were standing quite still, overcome by the immensity of the front hall.

They remained standing like that for one long spellbound moment. Emily, looking at them one by one, as though they were children in a painting, was certain that this was a picture she would be unlikely to see again. All four standing still and in silence! It was almost unheard of.

They each had brown hair, although Jean's was almost black and Ann's had a glimmer of red and a touch of gold combined in it. Both boys had brown eyes and both girls blue.

John had a thin serious face, not unlike Emily's own. He looked older than seven and was full of questions as he studied this strange house. He was holding something—wrapped loosely against the wind and rain—in his two hands. Through an opening in the cloth covering, Emily glimpsed the bars of a cage. She wondered if her mother had noticed this yet.

James, already getting over his feeling of strangeness and beginning to move, was stockier than his older brother. His face was rounder and, somehow, especially alive. Emily remembered the stories she had heard about James. He grinned at her unexpectedly, and she decided, even as he looked quickly away, that he would be fun to know.

Jean was small and dreamy. She stood as close to her father as she could get.

"I'm four, aren't I, Daddy?" she said in a thin voice.

"You are indeed," Uncle Roger assured her, swinging her up into the safety of his arms.

Ann had no intention of letting Jean take first place.

"I'm free! I'm free!" she clamored, tugging at her father's coat. "Pick me up too."

Uncle Roger obediently shifted Jean to one arm and scooped Ann up as well.

"All right, you're three," he agreed. "Now how about all of you saying hello to these people."

"Hello," the four children mumbled, ducking their heads and looking anywhere but at the Blairs.

Then John recalled his position as eldest.

"I don't believe you've met my gerbil, Aunt Elizabeth," he said politely, whisking the cover off the cage. "She's a Mongolian mouse and her name is Daisy."

Mother flattened against the wall as he came toward her.

"Don't you like gerbils?" he asked, studying her horrified face with surprise. "Mother says she's grown quite fond of Daisy."

"Good for Mother," Mrs. Blair said hollowly. Then, taking a deep breath, she peered into the cage.

"Lovely. . . just lovely, John," she managed to say. "Does she stay in that cage all the time?"

"Every single minute," Uncle Roger said before John could answer. "And see you remember that, John."

"But, Daddy, she's used to having her exercise," John protested.

"She can get all the exercise she needs on her treadmill. That's an order," Uncle Roger said.

John said, "Yes, sir," meekly—but Emily happened to be watching James. His eyes were gleaming. She had an uneasy feeling that Uncle Roger had given his order to the wrong boy.

4

"It IS Haunted!"

The boys and Daisy invaded the attic. It had been, for Emily, a domain of dreams. Now, as they ran from room to room, it crackled with life.

"Hey, John, let's try the bannisters!" James yelled.

Bang! Crash! Scramble! They were gone. Daisy, deserted in the bedroom which John had chosen, hunched in the bottom of her cage and looked worried.

"It's okay, Daisy. They'll be back," Emily said, to comfort her. Or was that what the gerbil wanted to hear?

The girls were calling from the foot of the

stairs. They led Emily proudly to the enormous bedroom they were to share.

"It's beautiful," Emily agreed, seeing the clean baseboard, the shining windowsills she had had to wash three times over.

"Peter! PETER!"

"That's Mother," Emily said, stiffening.

"She's scared," Ann stated.

"Peter!" Mother called again.

Emily and Mr. Blair reached Mrs. Blair at the same moment. She was standing in the middle of the front hall downstairs. She laughed unsteadily when she saw their anxious faces, but she had to swallow before she could speak.

"I . . . it's so silly really . . . I heard a noise," she said.

"A noise?" Dad said, staring at her. "What sort of noise?"

"I was in the kitchen," she explained carefully. "I was just standing there looking around, not touching anything. I wasn't even near anything, Peter."

"All right," he said, trying to calm her. "What happened?"

"All of a sudden there was a moan. Honestly, it sounded exactly like a moan. But I was the only person there."

The little girls had joined them now. They looked up at their aunt with wide, solemn eyes.

"It must have been the wind," Dad said, as though his wife were Jean's age.

"No, it was a moan," Mother was stubborn. "I admit it sounds silly now, but—"

"Let's go and see," Dad suggested. He sounded fatherly, a little amused.

The five of them trooped out to the kitchen. They stood just inside the doorway and listened. There was no sound. Emily tried to breathe more quietly. She glanced at her mother. Mother was waiting, listening intently.

Then Jean said shakily, "Is that a monster breathing?"

They all heard it in the same instant. Someone was panting loudly. Emily, her nerves tightening, looked hastily around at the others. Nobody was breathing. Still the panting went on. It did not come from their direction. It was simply there, filling the room, coming out of the air.

"What on earth—" Dad began, almost whispering.

Then the thing moaned.

"OoooooooooooooooOOO!" it cried eerily.

"There, Peter, I told you so," Elizabeth Blair said.

Emily took a step nearer her father in spite of herself.

Jean simply screamed. Her scream was every bit as terrifying as the mysterious moan had been. It split the air and shattered what little calm the others had left.

But, in the moment of silence following her shriek, they all heard James's voice say clearly, "John, what was that?"

They froze in their places.

There was a mutter of another voice, and then James spoke again. "But there's nobody here but us. Is there anybody here?" he roared suddenly.

Uncle Roger arrived in time to hear him.

"Where are the boys?" he said, looking around.

"They're not here," Mother told him. "We're the only ones here."

Uncle Roger looked at her in surprise.

"But I heard James speak," he said reasonably. "James, where are you?"

The breathing sounded again for a moment. Then James, clearly on the verge of tears, replied shakily, "Daddy, is that you?"

"Of course it's me"—Uncle Roger was getting annoyed— "and I asked you a question, young man. Now come out from wherever you're hiding."

They all looked around the kitchen as he spoke. There was no hiding place except in the pantry. James's voice did not come from the pantry.

"I'm not hiding," James said.

"WHERE ARE YOU, JAMES?" Uncle Roger thundered.

"I'm up in the closet talking into the little phone," James howled.

"Let me, stupid," John said.

There were sounds of a scuffle.

"Dad?" John asked.

"Yes." Uncle Roger's voice shook, but whether

it was from anger or from laughter Emily could not tell.

"We're upstairs in a big closet, like a room, and there's this thing on the wall, like a mouthpiece, and we were trying it out. Where are you?"

"In the kitchen . . . just a minute." Uncle Roger had begun to walk toward the sound. "Keep talking, John."

"What'll I say?"

"Never mind. I've found it."

The children's father turned to the rest of them with a broad smile.

"Look," he said.

It was right there in the wall, a round mouthpiece. They would have seen it sooner except it was hidden in the space between the cupboards and the refrigerator.

"Well, I'll be," Peter Blair said. He turned to his wife. "You almost had me believing the place was haunted, Elizabeth."

"Had *you* believing it!" Mother shuddered. "You should have been out here, all by yourself, and heard that moan. I was ready to pack up and leave then and there!"

"It's a speaking tube," Uncle Roger said, examining it with interest. "It's so the lady of the house can talk to the cook, I suppose, or so the housemaid can call up and tell her who's at the front door."

"That will be the day!" Mother said.

"Where is it? Where is it?"

The boys burst into the kitchen.

"Boy, what a neat thing for sending secret messages!" John said, pushing James away and standing on his toes to get near the mouthpiece.

"Hello . . . hello . . . hello. . . testing . . . testing one, two, three," he called into it. "Hey, James, go back to the other one."

James was off like a flash.

"I want to try it. Daddy, what is it? Let me try it too," Jean demanded.

"It's my turn," Ann said.

"Your turn to what?" Emily asked her.

"What Jean said," Ann answered, not about to miss anything.

"Girls, I need you to help unpack. Teddy and Henriette are still in the station wagon," Uncle Roger told them.

A moment later the three Blairs were alone. John was so busy talking to James he might have been in another world.

"This is Captain X calling. We need reinforcements down here," Emily heard him growl in a deep voice.

"Peter," Mother said, running one hand through her dark hair and leaning against her husband's shoulder, "how does Roger do it?"

"He's used to them." Dad laughed.

He put his arm around her and held her up.

"This day . . . I don't know how I'll ever get through it!" Mother went on. "If one more thing happens, just one more thing—"

"James wants his bedroom painted black," Emily told her with a grin. "He said so upstairs."

"BLACK!" Mother shrieked. She straightened and flung her hands wide in despair. "Now that was exactly what I needed to hear! Black! With purple woodwork?"

"No, just plain black," Emily said. "He wants it mysterious, like a robber's den."

"How has Deborah kept from having TB long ago?" Mother asked them. "I don't expect to survive the first week."

Emily burst out laughing.

"Emily Blair, have you no heart?" Mother cried.

Emily simply shook her head. Whatever her mother said—in spite of the gerbil and the huge house and the children and the rain and the ghost—Emily knew in that instant that her mother was enjoying herself.

It seemed years later before all four Sutherland children were in bed. Even though it was fun, it was wearing. The noise, for one thing! Emily had never lived in the middle of so much hubbub before.

"You go on up too, Emily," her mother said, catching sight of her weary face.

"It's only eight thirty!" Emily protested half-heartedly.

"It feels like four in the morning," Mother said.

Emily, beginning to drag her feet in the direction of the stairs, almost missed hearing her add, "Let's say good night here. I can't face climbing to that attic."

The box! Emily thought jubilantly. At last!

Keeping her eyes lowered, she kissed both her parents. She walked away from them, walked as though her muscles ached, walked as though she were tired out. But when she rounded the first landing, she began to hurry, and she fairly sped up the last flight.

In her room, though, with the door closed, with the box actually in her hands, Emily did not know what to do. She had hoped that the key would come to light while she and her mother housecleaned, but there had been no sign of it.

Maybe if she shook the box. She tried. It stayed locked. She pried at the lid. She tried using a straightened-out paper clip as a key. Nothing worked.

"But I've been waiting so long!" she protested, as though someone were arguing with her. "I have to know what's in it . . . even if I have to break it open."

Silence answered her. In that silence, she heard a girl's voice warning her: *O, intruder, beware of the beast!*

Emily was not afraid of any beast, but she knew that she did not want to be that intruder.

I'd have to use the hatchet, she thought.

That ended that. The box was old. The finish was off the back of it. But it was still a special box, a secret box, a box to be respected.

Emily scowled. She wanted so badly to know

what was inside. Losing hope, she turned the box around once more in her hands.

Then she saw it—a corner of paper sticking out from under the edge of the lid. It had not been there before, she was sure. She must have jiggled it out. Maybe . . . just maybe . . .

She pulled on it with trembling fingers. Carefully, carefully! It must not tear. It snagged, and she thought she would not be able to free it. Then it came. It was in her hands, a piece of paper, folded in four.

Emily took a deep breath, wished desperately for it to be something that mattered, and unfolded it.

She recognized Kate's spiky writing at once.

When I opened my eyes this morning,
The day belonged to me.
The sky was mine and the sun,
And my feet got up dancing.
The marmalade was mine and the squares of
    sidewalk
And all the birds in the trees.
So I stood and I considered
Stopping the world right there,
Making today go on and on forever.
But I decided not to.
I let the world spin on and I went to school.
I almost did it, but then, I said to myself,
"Who knows what you might be missing
    tomorrow?"

"Poems," Emily said softly. She read the words again. "Oh, Kate," she murmured.

Deliberately, she refolded the piece of paper and slid it back into the locked box. She pushed it all the way in so that she would not be able to get it and read it again. Then she put the box behind the books in the bottom shelf of her bookcase.

As she undressed and climbed into bed, she knew she and Kate were going to be friends. She had no idea when it would happen or how. But if the box held more poems, as Emily was sure it must, Kate was bound to come and find her. From that first moment when they met, they would be friends. Not like Ruth and Moira and Sharon! Real friends.

"'And my feet got up dancing,'" Emily said over to herself and smiled.

They were friends already except that Kate did not yet know it.

And I'm sleeping in my new room, she realized.

She was wide awake all at once. She tried to hold on to Kate's happy words but they escaped, leaving her alone in the darkness. In the apartment, when she had been in bed, she had always been able to hear her parents in the living room. Here she lay in a great silence. Suddenly she remembered the moaning in the kitchen. Telling herself it had only been James did not help. She breathed shallowly and tried to ward off the fear that rushed at her.

Then she heard a scurry of small feet in John's room. Daisy was awake too, running on her treadmill. It squeaked annoyingly, but Emily, coming out of her moment of panic, was grateful.

Her eyes were used to the darkness now. She looked up through her casement window. A star was looking in at her. One small silver star, shining directly at her, giving her courage!

Emily lay and watched it. She thought of all she had learned about stars in school. None of it made any difference. Though her reason told her she was wrong, she was certain the star knew she was there and that it was shining especially brightly just for her.

Then she, too, made a poem. It was only a small one, and she did not bother getting up to write it down. It would keep inside her head till morning.

Far above my town,
A silver star shines down.
It smiles in through my pane
And I smile back again.
I feel scared and small,
Not grown-up at all,
But it shines down at me
So very steadily.
While I watch its spark,
I do not mind the dark.

5

Mrs. Thurstone
Comes To Call

"Dad, who lives around here?" Emily asked
next morning at breakfast. She spread
honey on her toast while she waited for his
answer. She did not want to have to explain her
excitement if he should mention Lindsay or
Kate.

"Old Mrs. Thurstone lives next door," her
father said. "She lives alone, in that stone house
with the lions for gateposts."

Emily was disappointed but interested too.

"But, Peter, that place is even bigger than
this," Mother objected.

"I know it. And she's over eighty. But she won't move. And she won't have any of her family live with her. I've met her nephew. She's quite a worry to them."

"But how does she manage?"

"Her food is delivered to the house. She gets it ready herself. She must have shut off most of the rooms. She's eccentric, to say the least."

"I saw her yesterday, looking out her window at me," Jean said unexpectedly, her eyes bright with terror. "She's a witch, isn't she, Uncle Peter?"

Dad laughed at her.

"No, she's simply an old lady who likes to live her own life in her own way. I say more power to her! But she's not my relative, which simplifies things. Don't expect her to drop in and welcome you to the neighborhood," he told his wife.

It was Emily who answered the doorbell an hour later and found the old lady herself standing on the step.

She was dressed entirely in black. She even wore a large black hat, with limp plumes curling over its brim. Her face was small, brown and creased like a walnut. Her eyebrows bristled alarmingly and both her nose and chin were formidable. Her black eyes fixed Emily in place as though they were thumbtacks. Emily simply stared.

"Well, girl, cat got your tongue?" she snapped in a rusty voice as fierce as an eagle's swoop. "I've come to call. Invite me in!"

Emily recovered her wits.

"Oh, I'm sorry," she stammered. "Come in, please. I'll get Mother."

The elderly lady, leaning on an ebony cane, hobbled into the hall. Putting out the hook of her cane, she caught the girl as she turned to go. "Where's that tribe of little hellions you keep here?" she asked. "I saw them come yesterday. Car left this morning, but they didn't. See they're out of the way. I don't like children. Never did."

"They're upstairs watching the painters," Emily said.

She did not defend her cousins. Old Mrs. Thurstone sounded so sure they were hellions that Emily was prepared to take her word for it. She turned again to go in search of her mother but, once more, the crook of the cane held her.

"Hoity-toity, girl. I'm eighty-seven years old. Show me to a chair, if you please!"

Emily led her into the living room. Mrs. Thurstone peered around at the Blair's couch and chairs that seemed lost in the large room.

"Humph," she snorted, "just as I thought. People today don't know . . ."

But Emily had fled.

She could not resist coming back with her mother, however. Mrs. Thurstone motioned them to chairs with a queenly wave of her stick.

"For all the world as though *we* were visiting *her*," Mother told Dad later.

Questions came thick and fast. Who were the

Blairs? Mrs. Thurstone had never heard of any Riverside Blairs.

"They lived on Snow Street," Mother said.

"Oh, well, that explains it. I know nobody on Snow Street," the old lady said grandly.

But she went on, wanting to know about Mother's family, who the children were, how much the Blairs had paid for the house, how much Peter Blair was paid.

At that, Mother's chin went up a notch. Her eyes flashed.

"Really, Mrs. Thurstone, that is an impertinent question!" she spluttered.

The old lady gave a cackle of laughter.

"Of course it is," she agreed. "Wanted to see if you'd be fool enough to answer it. None of my business! I don't want that tribe of youngsters setting foot on my property, young woman, do you hear?"

Emily was so rattled by the abrupt turn the conversation had taken that words jumped out of her mouth before she could stop them. "They won't," she assured their guest. "They think you're a witch."

Mother gave Emily a scathing look, but Mrs. Thurstone cackled again.

"Good," she said. "Maybe I *am* a witch. Did you ever think of that, girl? Tell them I said so. What's that noise?"

The other two looked blankly at her. The old lady cocked her head on one side.

"Rain," she said decidedly. "But it isn't raining."

Then the Blairs heard it too—water falling steadily. Automatically they looked at the window framing the bright July morning.

"It's here in the house," Mrs. Thurstone told them impatiently. "I may be eighty-seven, but I haven't lost all my faculties."

Emily and her mother got up and hurried to the door. Now they could see the "rain." Incredibly, a definite wall of water was falling through the bannisters from the floor above.

"What have they done?" Elizabeth Blair gasped, and they ran for the stairs.

The water came from one of the unused bedrooms. Emily was already barefoot. Mother took only a second to kick off her shoes. Side by side, they waded into the room. John, James, Jean, and Ann were standing in a row, directly across from them, watching the water flow by.

"Where is it coming from?" Mother shouted at them.

Before they could explain, she had seen for herself. The cap was missing from the valve of the radiator. Mother splashed over and put her hand on the opening. The spurt of water stopped.

She stared at the children. They stared back. Nobody spoke. Then, as Mother opened her mouth to begin, Jean burst into tears. Emily's soft heart was smitten. Mother had a harder heart.

"Emily, leave her alone. Jean, stop that! Water is one thing we don't need. Where's the thing you screw on to stop this?"

There was a profound silence. Jean's sobs dwindled slowly to sniffles. The three older children all looked at Ann.

"Where'd you put it?" John demanded.

"What?" Ann answered, as though she had trouble hearing.

"Where'd you put the thing that keeps the water in?" he barked at her.

"What?" Ann said again, putting her thumb in her mouth and looking as though she did not understand the language they were speaking.

Mother's patience wore thin.

"Did Ann take it?"

"Yes," the others cried. "She came to get us because she said we could sail boats."

"Sail boats!" Taking a deep breath, Mother turned to face Ann directly. As she moved, her hand slipped. The water spurted again.

"Damn!" Elizabeth Blair said, between set teeth—and put her hand back. She rounded again on Ann, taking care not to move her hand as she did so.

"Ann, listen to me. And don't say 'What?' "

"Okay," Ann said, removing her thumb from her mouth.

"Where is the thing that keeps the water in?"

"Does James have it?" Ann wanted to know. She spoke pleasantly but her voice trembled.

"No, I don't!" James yelled at her. He was so often in trouble. He had an idea he was not clear of trouble now, but one thing he did not have, and that was the cap for the radiator. "It was gone when I came."

Ann straightened suddenly and faced her aunt.

"I know where it is," she announced.

"Where?"

"Yonder in the bushes," Ann said, waving at the opposite wall. "It's yonder in the bushes."

"Yonder in WHAT bushes?"

Mother was almost screaming. She looked as though she were caught in a nightmare. Her hair stood on end. The hand not holding back the water shook.

"Yonder in the bushes," Ann repeated, crestfallen but obstinate. Her thumb went back in her mouth.

For an instant they stood there helplessly. Then a creaky old voice, speaking from the doorway, jolted sense back into them.

"The child's forgotten where she put it, girl," Mrs. Thurstone told Mother. The old lady was out of breath, but her eyes gleamed with excitement. "Look for it, you little fools. You." She pointed her stick at Emily.

"Me?" Emily gasped.

"Go and search her room. That's where it'll be, mark my words. You should never leave a child to her own devices."

Emily found the radiator cap under Ann's pillow. As she snatched it up and ran to her mother, she heard once again the cracked old voice saying, "Maybe I *am* a witch. Did you ever think of that, girl?"

Mother screwed the cap back in place. The flood was over—over except for the gallons of water on the floor.

Jean and Ann were sent to their room to think. The boys had to help clean up. Mrs. Thurstone stayed to watch, giving quantities of advice whenever she thought they needed it. It took over an hour.

"What you need is a hired girl," she told Mrs. Blair, when they had wrung out the mop for the last time and gone back downstairs.

"Oh, Mrs. Thurstone, what I wouldn't give for a hired girl," Mother said, with longing in her voice. "But picture the ad."

WANTED: One hired girl, to cook, clean, wash, iron, make beds, do dishes, etc., in house with eighteen rooms and five children.

"In *my* day—" Mrs. Thurstone started.

"But your day is no more." Mother sank into a chair though the old lady still stood upright, supported by her stick. "Such a person does not exist—and I don't blame her. This job ages you. I feel one hundred and eighty-seven this minute!"

A new expression flickered across the old lady's seamed face and vanished. Seconds later it dawned on an amazed Emily that she had seen old Mrs. Thurstone smile.

"Stuff and nonsense," Mrs. Thurstone said briskly to the younger woman. "You're thriving on all this. It's becoming to you. Good day."

She was almost out the door before the Blairs realized she was leaving. They hurried after her to bid her good-bye properly, but she waved them away and, half-striding, half-tottering, crossed the lawns to her own house.

Mother and daughter turned back and faced each other. Suddenly, helplessly, the two of them were swept away on a wave of laughter.

"Oh," Emily moaned, clutching her aching sides.

Mrs. Blair wiped her eyes and struggled to stop. Then in spite of herself, she gasped, "It's yonder in the bushes, Emily. Yonder in the bushes."

"Stuff and nonsense," Emily choked.

And they laughed harder than ever.

6

Sophie

Emily wakened every morning determined to find out something about Lindsay and Kate before night. But there was no time.

"Work, work, work—that's all we ever do," she complained.

"I know," her mother said. "But think of all the valuable experience you're getting."

"I'd rather wait till I'm older," Emily told her.

"Me too," said Elizabeth Blair.

So Emily went on making beds, hanging out washing, drying dishes, making peanut-butter sandwiches, and trying to keep track of John, James, Jean, and Ann. She did not even have enough time to herself for making up poems—

in spite of having her room in a garret. Sometimes, when she was in bed, she would start a verse, but she would be so tired she fell asleep before she had done more than a line or two. She did complete one short rhyme. She herself was surprised by it. She had started it as a complaint about the kind of life she was living now compared to the peaceful years she had spent with her parents in an apartment. But it came out differently than she planned. She showed it to her mother.

When I was an only child,
Life was nice and neat and mild.
Now that I am one of five
It's harder—but it's more alive.
Everything was easy then
But I would not go back again.
Being one of five's more fun
Than being just the only one.

Mrs. Blair laughed when she read it.

"It is more alive," she agreed. She had broken up two wrestling matches since lunch. "But we had fun when there were only the three of us, didn't we?"

Emily nodded, thinking back. They had read books together. They had talked and gone for walks and attended concerts. It had been a different kind of fun, that was all.

"Emily." Her mother interrupted her train of

thought. "I need some groceries—a loaf of bread and an extra package of hot dogs. And the painters have given me notice that unless I remove James they plan to go on strike. Could you take him with you and go to the store?"

"Okay," Emily agreed, still thinking about her poem.

"You wouldn't consider taking all four and buying them Popsicles?"

"Oh, Mother!"

"Here's the money," Mrs. Blair said quickly. "They're already outside, waiting for you."

Mother did look tired, Emily thought as she struggled to keep her charges on the sidewalk and all headed in the right direction. She felt she had won a major victory when all of them, Popsicles in hand, emerged from the store without anything dire happening.

"Emily, it's pouring down rain," James pointed out. They huddled back under the store awning.

"It's raining. It's pouring. The old man is snoring . . ." the little girls chanted.

"Rats!" Emily said. There had been no sign of rain when they left home half an hour ago.

"Would you kids like a ride?" a tall girl came over to ask.

She had left the store just ahead of them, Emily remembered. She looked doubtfully at the stranger. Emily was not supposed to accept rides from people she did not know, but the rain was pelting down now.

"It's all right, really. I live just down the street from you—or my family does anyway. Aren't you Mr. Blair's children?"

"I am." Emily relaxed a little. "These are my cousins."

"Well, I'm Laurel Ross. And there's room for all of you in the car if you squeeze a bit. I even have an account in your father's bank—if that makes me a friend."

Emily grinned in relief.

"This way." Laurel beckoned, and they made a dash through the downpour.

A tall, gangly boy was sitting in the car, waiting.

"This is my brother James," Laurel said as they piled in, trampling on each other, squealing at the wet.

"This is *my* brother James," John said, laughing and pointing.

"What?" the boy said.

"Oh." Laurel laughed, understanding. "They have a James too," she explained to her brother.

"Ann, don't let your Popsicle melt in here!" Emily wailed, suddenly the anxious mother. "Eat it quick!"

"It's okay," Laurel reassured her. "We're almost there."

Then Emily straightened and stared intently at the back of the tall, dark girl's head.

"Did you say your name is Laurel Ross?" she asked.

"That's what I said."

"Do you know a girl called Lindsay Jane Ross?"

"Know her! She's our sister," Laurel returned. "But how do you know Lindsay? She's been away at the cottage since before you arrived."

"I . . . I just heard her name mentioned," Emily stammered.

She wanted desperately to ask more questions, but she did not know where to begin. The car had stopped now. Mother was holding the door open for them.

"Do you know a girl named Kate?" Emily blurted out.

"Hurry *up*, Emily. Move!"

"Kate is Lindsay's best friend," Laurel said.

She turned in the front seat so that she could see Emily's face. But suddenly Ann tripped getting out of the car. She fell flat on her face on the gravel drive. What was left of her Popsicle flew out of her hand and landed in a puddle. Questions were forgotten as Laurel and Emily both sprang to her rescue. Carrying her, they ran for the house. James Ross waited in the car.

"Won't you stay for a cup of tea or something?" Mother invited Laurel. "And thank you so much for bringing them home. I'd never have sent them if I'd guessed this deluge was about to break."

"No, we can't—though we'd like to," Laurel said politely, handing Ann over. "I'm due back in Toronto tonight, and my mother is waiting for the groceries we bought."

Emily followed her to the door.

"It's a shame both Kate and Lindsay are away," Laurel said, just as Emily was wondering how to begin.

"When will they be back?"

"Not till school starts. At least Lin won't, and I'm pretty sure Kate's away all July and August too. They're quite a pair."

What do you mean ? Emily longed to ask, but Laurel smiled good-bye and ran back to her car.

"What a lovely girl," Mother said, putting Ann down.

Emily could not answer. Kate would not be coming for the box for six weeks! Six weeks! How was she, Emily, going to bear it?

An hour later, when the storm had blown over and the children had gone out to play in the wet garden, the front doorbell jangled.

"You go," Mother said. "Who knows? It might be Mrs. Thurstone."

"It couldn't be," Emily said.

Not really caring, she swung back the door and came face to face with Mrs. Thurstone herself, black hat, ebony stick, and all. Only this time she had someone with her, a girl with a suitcase. And the girl was crying!

"Don't stand there gaping like a goldfish," the old lady barked. "Fetch your mother."

Emily turned and ran.

"It *is* Mrs. Thurstone," she gasped. "And she's got a girl with her and the girl's crying and she wants you."

"What now?" Mother said and took off her apron.

When Mrs. Blair and Emily reached her, Mrs. Thurstone had marched into the house, bringing the stranger along. The two of them stood in the front hall.

"Why, Mrs. Thurstone, how nice—" Mother started.

"Don't be daft," was all the old lady said to that, but it stopped the other woman's speech of welcome abruptly.

"There she is," the old lady announced then. Triumphantly, she pointed her cane at the girl who had come with her.

The girl sobbed. The Blairs stared at her, unable to stop themselves. She was young, not yet twenty. Her lipstick was smudged. Her long, corn-colored hair was pulled back into an untidy knot. Her hands twisted together. Her face was swollen from crying. She looked frightened out of her wits.

Neither Mother nor Emily had any idea who she was or why she was there.

Mrs. Thurstone, seeing their bewilderment, explained.

"She's your hired girl," she announced, as if that settled the matter. "I don't want her—and she has nowhere else to go."

"I'm afraid I don't understand," Mother said. "Won't both of you come in and sit down?"

Emily felt sorry for her mother. Mrs. Thurstone

sailed ahead of them into the living room. She lowered herself gingerly into the least comfortable chair, gestured to the girl to sit on the couch, and waited for the other two to sit down.

Then she told the story. The girl's name was Sophie Tremblay. She was from Belgium, and she spoke Flemish and French. She knew only a little English.

"Her brother Jacques brought her out to Canada about a year ago," the old lady went on, speaking about Sophie as though she were not sitting right there with them. "She kept house for him in Toronto. She was shy and made no friends. Then Jacques decided to get married to some girl he met at the factory. So he took this child to an employment agency and asked them to find her a job where she could 'live in.' I gather he's a regular prince among men," Mrs. Thurstone commented grimly at this point.

"But how—" Mother began.

"My niece Annabelle had the temerity to ask at the agency for somebody to live with her great-aunt." The old lady snorted. "The woman thought this girl was just what Annabelle had in mind. You see, I speak French," she added, making things clearer. "My husband and I lived in Paris for some time, forty years ago."

Emily stared at the old woman who said this so casually. She had a sudden vision of Mrs. Thurstone in Paris, a much younger and very shadowy Mrs. Thurstone but with all the present Mrs. Thurstone's fire and spirit. She felt sure there would be people in Paris who still remembered her.

"So Annabelle drove up and deposited the girl on my doorstep. 'I won't take No for an answer, Aunt Anne,' says she. 'We'll pay all her expenses, and we'll feel so much happier knowing you're being properly cared for.'"

The old lady chuckled wickedly.

"So I didn't say No. I let her drive off thinking she'd got her own way—Miss Uppity!—because I thought of you. She's exactly the person you need. She's seventeen. She knows how to work hard. And she's lonely. This is just the place for her."

Mother gathered her scattered wits.

"But, Mrs. Thurstone, we couldn't possibly interfere. Your niece is right—"

"I'll thank you to mind your own affairs, young lady." Mrs. Thurstone glared. "When I need a keeper, I'll choose my own. I'll tell Annabelle you're keeping an eye on me, if it will make you feel better. You can do it too," she added surprisingly. "I'll call you each morning and, if I don't, you can come and fetch the doctor or the undertaker, if need be. But meanwhile I don't intend to be bothered with the likes of her. Told her so. That's what made her cry. Poor child doesn't know whether she's on her head or her heels," she finished.

The crustiness vanished for a moment, with the last few words. Emily was startled by the knowledge that she might, someday, even love this cantankerous old lady. Already she was glad she knew her.

"She may even teach your children some French," Mrs. Thurstone put in slyly. "Isn't that the latest thing for parents to want in this bilingual country? Ha!"

Emily could not decide what the "Ha!" meant, but she did know the old lady was right. She had heard her parents talk of how little French they knew, how much they hoped Emily would learn to speak it fluently. It was an important part of being a Canadian, her father had said.

"But have you told her—" Mother began.

"I've told her everything. Told her you had four little demons over here and a big girl who should be more help. Told her your husband was fool enough to buy a house he couldn't afford. Told her you don't know where to turn and you need someone who knows what real work is. Didn't tell her you weren't overly bright. She can find that out for herself. She's overjoyed at the idea. She's crying now because she thinks you'll send her away. Or maybe she's afraid I'll change my mind and keep her after all. She's scared to death of me," old Mrs. Thurstone boasted.

Mother turned to Sophie and looked directly into the honest, frightened eyes.

"Sophie," she said slowly, "would you like to work here?"

"Oh, *oui, madame,*" the girl breathed, clasping her hands in entreaty. "I work very hard!"

"But she's only a child," Mother cried suddenly, moving over and putting her arm around Sophie's shoulders protectively. "She should still be in school."

"Fiddlesticks!" Mrs. Thurstone said tartly. "Put her to work and teach her English. Don't spoil her. And don't be running over for me to translate for you every other minute," she warned, getting to her feet with a grunt. "My life is quiet and I want it to stay that way!"

"Yes, Mrs. Thurstone," Mother said, as though she were Emily's age.

The old lady gave her a fierce look.

"And don't be impertinent," she snapped.

They all saw her to the door. Sophie's small suitcase stood in the hall. Mrs. Thurstone turned back for a final word.

"She loves children. Has seven younger brothers and sisters at home in Belgium. No wonder she left!"

She spoke to Sophie in rapid French. The girl babbled an answer, but Mrs. Thurstone cut it short and was off, her black skirts flapping, her cane rapping smartly along the verandah.

Mother, dismay written all over her, stood and stared at Sophie Tremblay.

"Why, we haven't even a bed for her!" she said.

"Never mind, Mother. Phone Dad. He'll get

one." Emily laughed. "Don't forget this is probably the only house in town where she can have her pick of four spare bedrooms."

7

A Friend for Sophie

Sophie borrowed Emily's bed that first night. Emily and the two small girls slept out in the backyard in a canvas tent Uncle Roger had brought from the farm. The tent really belonged to the two boys, and they had already spent several nights camping out in it. But Emily had never slept in a tent before.

It was queer and exciting. After Jean and Ann finally dropped off to sleep, Emily lay smelling the newly mown grass, the drift of sweetness from the lily-of-the-valley bed, the smell of the canvas itself. Car horns honked mysteriously, and crickets chirped in the darkness. A mosquito buzzed in, but Emily swatted him.

Suddenly she missed her star. Moving carefully, she crawled the length of her sleeping bag and unzipped the tent flap. She stuck her head out into the night. Thousands, millions of stars spangled the reaches of heaven. Emily felt lost for a moment. She could not find any pattern in the myriad points of light. Then she saw it.

"Hello, star," she said right out loud.

She watched it for a moment, making sure. Yes, it was off by itself, special, hers. It twinkled at her.

She ducked back into the tent.

The summer went on being "impossible." But Mother told Dad one night, "With Sophie, even the impossible is easier."

Daisy was lost, but Sophie found the gerbil before Mother discovered she had escaped. James had a nosebleed, but Sophie stopped it and cleaned him up, without speaking a word of English. She put the head back on Ann's teddy bear so that it stayed in place for days at a time. She worked in the garden—and knew weeds from flowers. While she washed dishes and made beds she sang, and she even hummed while she ironed.

"I'm getting the dusting done," Mother said, in wonder.

Still, Sophie was lonely. Sometimes, her voice cracked in the middle of a song and she was silent. More than once, after she had been up in her room, the family would see she had been crying. Emily, who was beginning to hunger for Kate or Lindsay or anybody her own age, felt especially close to the Belgian girl in her aloneness. But it was hard to know how to comfort her.

She tried asking Sophie to teach her some French. But Sophie did not want to speak French. She insisted Emily give her lessons in English instead. Ann was the only one who was learning any French, much to the disappointment of the adults. She followed Sophie around like a devoted shadow. As the days passed, she learned to say in perfect French "I am so slow!" "I have the head of a cabbage!" and "How stupid I am!" Sophie was forever scolding at herself for failing to understand everything immediately.

"Be patient with yourself, Sophie," Mother told her, smiling.

"Oui, madame," Sophie answered.

She did not smile though. She was sure she was more of a hindrance than a help to the Blairs, in spite of all she did each day. Even Mrs. Thurstone failed to talk sense into her.

"She needs . . . I don't know what she needs," Mother said in despair. "I'd like, just once, to see her completely happy. Not being brave, not pretending—just happy."

One morning, with no notion of what was about to happen, Mother herself sent the five children off to the park.

"Take care of them, Emily," she said, giving each of them a quarter to spend, "although the park should be safe enough."

"Okay, okay," Emily growled.

She had nothing better to do, but still, she was growing weary of being the built-in baby-sitter.

Nothing went wrong for the first hour. Then Jean had to go to the bathroom. Emily, having learned from experience how fatally easy it was to lose the Sutherland children when she had them out, gave the boys strict instructions not to stir while she took both little girls into the public washroom. When they came out, the boys had vanished.

Emily searched frantically. It was not a large park but there seemed endless clumps of trees the boys might be behind. They could not have left the park. Or could they? She grew desperate. She was about to go into a nearby house and phone her mother for help when she saw them running toward her.

"You . . . you . . ." she spluttered, so relieved to find them that she was beside herself with rage.

"Emily, wait!" James sobbed.

She looked at them then with eyes that really saw them. Both of them were panting. Their faces were flushed. James was crying openly, and John was struggling not to.

"What's the matter?"

They clutched at her hands and tugged her along with them as they explained. There was a big boy on the other side of the park. He had a kitten in a box, and he was going to drown it.

"Drown it?" Emily repeated, pulling back. "Where?"

But they only yanked harder at her. Now the little girls were as upset as the boys. Emily was carried along in spite of herself.

He was a big boy, she saw. He looked fifteen or sixteen. He was laughing as they came up to him.

"So it's my cat, kids," he taunted them. "And my dad said to get rid of it! How're you going to stop me?"

He had the kitten in a box in his bicycle basket. Emily could hear it crying.

"Emily will stop you," James said boldly.

Emily stared down at James. Then she saw the others' faces. All four of them were waiting for her to do something. Their tears had disappeared. They had managed to get her there in time. The kitten still lived. They trusted her, their big grown-up cousin, to fix things. Emily felt hollow.

"Are you really going to drown it?" she asked the boy weakly.

"Sure—or maybe wring its neck," the boy said.

Emily knew he was teasing, but the children gasped with new horror.

"Listen, nobody wants this cat . . . kitten. And I can do what I please with it. It's mine, not yours."

"Would you sell it?" Emily asked.

She was astonished at herself. The boy looked interested at once.

"What will you give me for it?"

Emily was about to offer first her own quarter and then raise the price bit by bit, but John volunteered, "We've each got twenty-five cents. Would that be enough?"

"Heck, that's nothing!" the boy jeered.

"That's all we have," John told him.

"A dollar and a quarter . . ." the boy said slowly.

A bigger boy whizzed by on a battered bicycle.

"Mom says come on home, Rick," he yelled. "It's twenty to twelve."

"Okay, here," the boy snapped.

James held out his hands for the box.

"Money first, kid," Rick told him flatly.

Emily counted the five quarters into his palm. He thrust the box at her.

"You better keep her shut up or she might get away on you," he said with a smirk. "She's too little to know any better."

As he took off, the children crowded around Emily. Each of them wanted to carry the box. Whatever was inside moved restlessly. The box felt heavy.

Maybe there's more than one, Emily thought. She pushed the idea out of her mind.

"I'll carry the box," she said firmly. "Let's go home."

They followed her as though she were the Pied Piper.

"What'll we name him?" John asked.

They all had suggestions. Tiger. Velvet. Fluffy. Patches.

Emily said nothing. She simply kept walking, walking toward home.

She won't let us keep him so there's no use thinking about it, she told herself sternly. But she said nothing to spoil the children's excitement. They would find out soon enough.

"We really should name him after somebody who almost drowned," John decided.

"I almost drowned once," James reminded him.

"Not you, dopey. Somebody famous!" scoffed his brother.

"His name is William Shakespeare," Emily announced.

She surprised herself as much as the Sutherlands.

"Why?" John asked for all of them.

"I don't know," Emily said. "It just is!"

But she did know. William Shakespeare was the grandest name she could think of. Even if Mother did make them give him up—and she would, Emily was certain—this small stray kitten would have had a proud name for a little while at least.

Kate would understand, she thought.

Nobody argued. Emily looked down at them, puzzled by their acceptance.

"Emily saved him," John told the others, "so she gets to choose."

The girls nodded solemnly. Jean reached out to touch the side of the box. James ran ahead of them and vaulted over a fire hydrant.

I should tell them, Emily thought miserably. It doesn't matter what his name is.

"We're home, kitten," Ann said.

Mrs. Blair met them in the hall. The children shouted with one voice, "We bought a kitten!"

They talked all at once, telling her the story of the rescue.

Mother set her jaw.

"Now, children—" she began.

"Wait, Aunt Elizabeth. Don't you want to see him?" they interrupted.

Emily opened the box.

William Shakespeare was no kitten. He was a cat, a scruffy, boney, striped cat, who crouched in the bottom of the box and glared up at them.

"He's not a kitten," Jean said.

The cat stood up and stretched.

"His back's thin and so's his tail, but his stomach isn't," Ann observed.

"He's not a 'he' at all," Mother snorted. "And she looks as though she's going to have kittens before long. I'll call the Humane Society right now."

"Mother, look how her bones stick out!" Emily cried, playing for time. "Can't we feed her first?"

"Well . . . she does look in need of a meal." Elizabeth Blair weakened. "But the moment she's through eating . . ."

Emily nodded. The cat allowed herself to be

picked up. Everyone, Mrs. Blair included, went to the kitchen. And there, Sophie and Willie met.

The moment the Belgian girl saw the scrawny cat huddled in Emily's arms she burst into a torrent of delighted French.

Mother struggled to translate.

"I think . . . maybe . . . she had a cat like this at home," she told the wide-eyed children. "Oh, dear, she thinks we're going to keep her. Emily, don't . . ."

Emily paid no attention to her mother. She took a step forward and placed William Shakespeare in Sophie's outstretched arms.

"We cannot have a cat on top of everything else." Mrs. Blair tried to make them listen. "Let alone kittens. Oh, look!"

The children were looking. And they knew— whatever Elizabeth Blair might be saying— Sophie and the cat had won the day.

The girl's face was radiant. She sank down onto the floor and sat cross-legged, making a nest of her lap. The battered, angular cat curled close to her. Suddenly, incredibly, the cat began to purr. Her purr rumbled hoarsely as though she were not used to using it. But it was a decidedly happy sound.

Sophie raised her head, her blue eyes alight.

"What is the name?" she asked Mrs. Blair.

"How . . . tell me . . . *how* does one explain the Humane Society to a Belgian-French maid, or whatever she is?" Mrs. Blair asked.

Nobody offered an answer.

"Sophie's happy now, Mother," Emily could not help saying.

Her mother gave her a squelching look.

"Thank you so much, Emily. I can see that. What is the creature's name?"

"William . . . I mean . . . Wilhelmina Shakespeare." Emily laughed.

Mother's lips twitched. She relayed the information to Sophie. Sophie shrugged her French shrug and went on stroking the cat tenderly.

"Willie, *ma petite*," she murmured.

Willie belonged.

8

Kate

"Another ten days and summer will be over," Mother said at the supper table.

"The 'impossible summer,'" Emily reminded her.

"Well, it has been!" Mother defended herself. "Take yesterday!"

The day before, the two boys had climbed out John's bedroom window and managed to get onto the roof of the house. Mrs. Thurstone had spotted them and called Mother. There they sat, side by side, on the peak of the roof, their eyes round with fright.

"Stay right there. Don't you dare move!" Mother called to them.

They had no intention of moving. The ground, three stories down, looked miles away. When the Fire Department came to the rescue, however, James started down to meet them. Emily gulped now, as she remembered seeing his feet slip and watching helplessly as he slithered all the way to the edge before his toes caught in the eaves trough.

"We have survived though, Elizabeth," Peter Blair pointed out.

"I may still be here, but I'm not the woman I was in June," Mother said darkly.

June seemed years ago to Emily. Her mother had said, then, that she was "terrified" of the Sutherland children and had agreed to take them "for the summer, at least" only because Uncle Roger and Aunt Deborah were desperate. Now, even though the summer was ending, Emily had no fear that Mother would send the children away. They sometimes did terrifying things, but she knew Mother was no longer in awe of them. They belonged to her just as Emily herself did.

Aunt Deborah will get better, an inner voice warned the girl.

Emily paid no attention. Her aunt's recovery was months away. She did not need to think about it yet.

She looked around at her cousins. John, his face intent, was putting relish on his second hot dog. Clearly it was important to get exactly the right amount of relish in exactly the right place.

James was already finishing his second hot dog, and while one hand was cramming the last mammoth bite into his mouth the other hand was reaching for his third. Jean was off in a world of her own, the first hot dog she had been given poised in her hand, halfway to her mouth, only two bites gone.

"Jean, eat!" Mother prompted.

Slowly, Jean raised the bun and took another nibble. Slowly, she began to chew. Mother turned away. Jean's jaw stopped moving.

Ann was burbling into her milk. She was doing it softly so that her aunt would not notice and tell her to stop. Her eyes gleamed wickedly at Emily over the rim of her cup.

Suddenly, Emily became aware that Mother was talking about the veterinarian.

"He told me the kittens aren't due for a week or two. He said she's an old hand at it—just leave things to her when the time comes."

"Don't forget to call me," Emily said.

"What are you going to contribute?" her mother wanted to know.

"I'm going to get my sex education." Emily grinned at her. "Dad's always saying kids should grow up on farms and see things get born. This is our chance."

"So now we're running a farm!" Mother said. "I keep promising myself that school will soon start and I'll just have the girls . . ."

"And Sophie and Willie," Emily added.

"And Daisy," put in John.

"Who on earth is Daisy?" Dad looked blankly from one to the other. "Have you taken in some other female and not even told me?"

The family was caught up in a whirlwind of laughter. Mother gasped out an explanation of Daisy's identity, and Dad, remembering, scowled at the lot of them. He could not keep it up though. In a moment he was laughing too. Sophie came flying from the kitchen, where she had been getting coffee, and stared around at them all as though they had lost their minds. Mother began to try to tell her what it was about, but before she had well begun, Sophie threw her hands up in the air, rolled her eyes, and went back to what she was doing.

That night, Emily lay in bed and thought about that burst of laughter. She and her mother and father—had they always laughed like that, all of a sudden, for no sensible reason? They had had good times together, she knew, but had they been silly together? She did not think so. Her father even kissed her mother differently now.

He used to do it . . . neatly, Emily thought, puzzling over the change. Now sometimes he looks as though he can't help it.

She smiled in the darkness, happy with her life as it was.

Now which would come first—Kate or the kittens?

They watched Wilhelmina closely as the days passed, but no kittens arrived. Finally September came. That last night before school began, Emily did not want to dry the supper dishes for Sophie. She did not want to help put one single, solitary child to bed. She wanted to escape, all alone, and brood about the coming day.

It was easier than she had imagined. The phone rang. Emily, slipping like a shadow across the hall, heard her mother say, "Of course, Dr. Maxwell. I'm thankful you called."

Me too, thought Emily as she eased open the front door.

She closed it behind her and stood still. She was free. That was one wonderful thing about this house. If someone called your name and you did not want to be discovered, you could simply not answer. Nobody would search eighteen rooms.

Emily sat on the wide front steps and looked out over the city. The last rays of the sun still caught the top of their hill, but below her, the houses were drowned in dusk. Was Kate down there somewhere? Emily stirred uneasily. The Kate she had imagined and come to like so much over the long weeks of summer—would she turn out to be real?

"Emily, Aunt Elizabeth sent me to tell you to give me a bath."

Emily gritted her teeth and turned to look at Jean.

"Where's Sophie?"

"She's gone over to Mrs. Thurstone's. Something's wrong with her."

Emily had no choice. Jumping to her feet, she grabbed the little girl's hand and dragged her all the way up to the third floor.

She turned on both taps full blast and, in a matter of seconds, whisked off Jean's clothes. The small girl stayed silent, head down. Emily, seething at having to be a nursemaid when all she wanted was to be left in peace, would not let herself wonder if something was wrong. Probably Jean just did not feel like talking. That suited Emily. She did not feel like talking either.

She lifted the little girl in over the side of the high tub and plunked her down in the water. At last, she was forced to look into Jean's face. The blue eyes were full of tears.

"Please, Emily, I'll bath my own self," she gulped. "I don't want you to have to bath me."

Emily hated herself. How could she explain? Jean had never been her age and afraid of starting at a strange school. Jean did not know what it was to feel imposed upon by her mother.

"I'm sorry," Emily said. "I didn't mean to be mean."

Jean smiled through her tears and forgave her on the spot. Emily felt more ashamed than ever.

When they were done, she wrapped Jean in a bath towel and carried her down the stairs. They met Emily's mother at the foot.

"She just needs her pajamas on and a book," Emily said.

"Oh, Emily, bless you," said her mother. "Could you manage to read to them too? I haven't finished clearing up the supper dishes and the boys need a hand."

Emily glowered. Then Ann came speeding into the hall, her yellow sleepers bright as a buttercup, her fat cheeks rosy.

"I want *Mrs. Tiggy Winkle*," she said.

"She always picks," Jean whined. "I don't want that stupid book."

"Perhaps Emily will read two," Mother said— and escaped.

Emily read two. The little girls, snuggling up to her, watching the pictures with such serious eyes, eased her anger. She turned the final page of *A Tree Is Nice* and sighed, as her listeners did, at the rightness of it.

Then she went back downstairs.

On the steps, it was darker now. Coming from the brightness of the lighted house, Emily could hardly see. She squinched up her eyes. Was that somebody standing on the lawn below her? It could not be. It must be simply a shadow. Nobody would stand there like that, in the dark, not saying a word.

"Hello," the shadow said, coming a step nearer.

"Hello," Emily returned faintly.

The shadow came closer still, and light from the windows turned the mysterious figure into a girl, taller than Emily, with a broad face and a boyish haircut.

"Who are you?" the girl asked.

Emily had been wondering the same thing about the other girl. Surely she, who lived in this house, should have been asking the questions. But something made her answer meekly.

"I'm Emily Blair. Who are you?"

The other girl moved away again into the darkening evening.

"Has your family really bought this place?" she asked, ignoring Emily's question.

"Yes," Emily answered, excitement rising in her. "We've been here since July. Do you live near here?"

"In the apartments down the street," the girl said. "Is the house really all painted and fixed up inside?"

"Of course it is."

Emily was growing surer now.

"What's your name?" she tried again.

"What room do you have?" the girl went on, as though it was terribly important.

She is! She must be! thought Emily.

Hanging onto her excitement, she managed to burst out, convincingly enough, "I don't even know your name. Why should I tell you—"

"My name's Kate Bloomfield," the girl said. "What room *do* you have?"

"The one in the attic, with the skylight and the casement window," Emily told her.

She said it as gently as she could and waited. Kate gave a queer little sigh and half turned so that Emily could no longer even see the faint glimmer that had been her face. There was silence between them.

I know you, Emily wanted to cry out. I know how you feel. I did find the box. It is all right. We're friends.

But this Kate was different. The words would not come.

"What does it matter?" Emily questioned instead, suddenly understanding that Kate, not she, would have to do the telling.

"I've been away all summer," Kate said. "They sent me to camp. I'm incorrigible. I wish you'd never come here, Emily Blair."

She ran away from Emily then, into the night.

Her swift steps halted.

"See you tomorrow," she called back.

Emily stood absolutely still on the step, staring after her. Had those last words been a promise—or a threat?

"Kate," she said once, quietly. But no one answered.

9

Half an Hour

The minute she walked into the classroom,
Emily saw Kate. In daylight, she looked
even more unlike Emily's dream of her than she
had the night before. She sprawled at her desk,
one elbow crooked over the chair back. She
was bragging about something, her head
thrown back.

I was so sure she'd have long hair, Emily
mourned. And I thought she'd be prettier.

Though Kate *was* pretty. Her deep-brown hair
glowed. Her dark eyes flashed. She shifted in
the chair and she moved easily.

She's like a boy, Emily thought.

As Emily took the place assigned to her, she,

all at once, thought of Kate's poem, the one she had managed to get out of the box.

Had Kate really written it? This Kate did not look like a girl who wrote poems. But there had been lines scratched out and new words inserted. It had looked like one of Emily's own poems before she had quite finished it. Or had she forgotten? Two months had gone by since she had unfolded that piece of paper.

> When I opened my eyes this morning,
> The day belonged to me.

That was how it had started.

Emily looked across at Kate again. Kate did look as though she might imagine she owned the day.

The other girl turned then and gave Emily back, stare for stare. Her eyes were cold. Emily shivered and busied herself arranging things in her desk.

"Would you pass out these papers, please, Lindsay?" Mr. Adamson asked.

The girl sitting right in front of Emily rose. She did not look one bit like Laurel Ross. She was small and fair. Still Emily knew, somehow, that whether they looked alike or not, this girl and Laurel were sisters. Lindsay's appearance did not disappoint her. Always Kate had been the one she had thought about, Kate who had written so blackly and clearly "O, intruder, beware of the beast!"

Neither of the girls spoke to Emily during school.

She was on her way home when Kate blocked the sidewalk in front of her.

"Emily Blair," she said.

Whether or not Kate wrote poems, she was half a head taller than Emily, and her eyes looked like splinters of ice.

"Yes," Emily said, standing her ground.

"You found the box, didn't you?"

"Yes," Emily said again.

"Did you open it?" Kate demanded.

"It's locked," Emily replied.

Kate must know it was locked. Why would she ask such a stupid question? Then Emily remembered thinking of taking the hatchet to it. She looked away, over Kate's head, but she could feel her cheeks grow hot.

"Okay." Kate relaxed a little. She still looked far from friendly. "I want it. I'll come over to your place in half an hour. You have it ready to hand over!"

"But what's in it?" Emily cried.

Kate glared at her.

"That has nothing to do with you, Emily Blair," she said. "You just have it ready when I get there."

She ran back toward the school. Emily turned and stared after her. Then she herself broke into a run. She had to get at what was in that box. She just had to! There must be a way. Maybe if she shook it again, she could get other papers to slide out. She had only half an hour. If she could just think of something!

She yanked open the front door and ran full tilt into her mother. Emily, in a hurry to get by, dodged, but Mrs. Blair caught her arm and held her fast.

"I have a job for you, Emily," she said.

"But, Mother, I have to . . ." Emily gasped, out of breath from her mad dash.

"You have to take Jean and Ann to the park and give them a swing. They've been begging to go all day long, and I promised them you'd take them the moment you got home."

Emily took a deep breath. This was her private affair, nothing to do with parents. Yet she could explain a little. Mother must understand.

"I have a friend coming over here in half an hour," she said.

Even if Kate did not like her, Emily had thought of her as a friend for so long that the words came naturally.

"You have two friends waiting for you in the backyard," her mother said. "One swing each and maybe a couple of slides and you can bring them back. What's your new friend's name?"

"Kate Bloomfield," Emily said dully.

"I'll tell Kate where you've gone. Why, Emily, you can be back by the time she gets here if you hurry. The girls have been so lonely today with the four of you gone. And Mrs. Thurstone sprained her wrist. Otherwise, I'd go. Emily, you know you love those children."

Emily stormed inwardly. Right now, at this

exact moment, she wished she were at the bottom of the sea.

"It's not fair!" she told her mother bitterly.

"I know it isn't," her mother said. "But life's full of unfair things—and they're waiting. We thought you'd come in the back way."

Emily slammed the door on her way out. The two little girls raced up to her.

"Emily, Emily," they screamed happily, "Aunt Elizabeth promised you'd take us to the park!"

"I'm big enough to go by myself really," Jean added. "But Ann's such a baby!"

"I am NOT a baby!" Ann stuck out her lip. "I'm big enough too."

The idea was there in Emily's mind without her having to think about it. She darted a look over her shoulder. Was her mother watching? There was no sign of her.

"Do you really think you could go by yourselves—" she began, her voice low.

"Oh yes, Emily. I know I can. I *know* it," Jean told her proudly.

"There's that one big street," Emily said.

"I know how to look both ways," Jean assured her. "I'd be *very* careful, Emily."

"I'd be very careful too," chimed in Ann.

"Well, if you start out, I'll catch up to you probably even before you get that far," Emily said. "There's something I want to get."

She could take the box with her. She could hide it in something and while the girls were sliding . . . That was the only way she would get to examine it again at all!

"Be terribly careful, Jean," she warned. "Are you sure you know the way?"

Jean simply looked scornful, and Emily had to admit it was a silly question. The park was straight down the street from their house. If only the girls did not have to cross Hedge Street.

Hand in hand, heads up, they set out. Emily could not watch. Unhappy but free, she ran back to the house, opened the side door as quietly as she could, listened till she heard noises in the kitchen, and went swiftly and soundlessly up the back stairs.

A moment later, the box was in her hands. As soon as she picked it up, she knew her idea was useless. It was locked against her as securely as ever. She shook it hopefully, but no edge of paper appeared. And the little girls were out on the street all by themselves.

Emily dropped the box on her bed, in plain sight of anyone who chanced into her room, and started down the stairs as quietly as she had come up. She had only been a minute. Probably Jean and Ann had not even reached the first corner yet. Listening for her mother, she neared the bottom step.

But it was not her mother she heard. She was at the foot of the stairs when the front door banged open and she heard Jean.

"I killed Ann!" Jean was crying, her voice wild with a horror too great for a four-year-old to handle. "Ann's dead! Ann's dead!"

10

After the Accident

Mother reached Jean first and caught her up in her arms.

"Jeanie, what are you saying?" she demanded. "Where is Ann?"

But Emily did not wait for her small cousin to sob out an explanation. She was out the door, running for the park. Almost at once she saw the knot of people gathered, the car stopped in the middle of the road.

"Let her be all right! Please, please, let her be all right," she begged as she ran. She could not really believe that Ann, so alive, so much herself just a few minutes before, could really have been killed. Yet she was more afraid than she had ever been in her life. The ugly fact that, whatever had happened, she, Emily, was at fault, she held away from her, unable to bear everything at once.

As she reached the people, she stopped short, closed her eyes, opened them, and pushed her way through.

"Hi, Emily," Ann said. "I ran into a car."

Emily, her knees shaking, sank down beside the small girl. Ann was not dead. But her face was scraped. And she was leaning against a young man Emily had never seen before.

"Do you know her?" he said. "I didn't really hit her. I don't think she's seriously hurt. She just dashed out into the side of my car as I drove past the corner."

"Jean wanted to hold my hand," Ann explained, her voice shrill suddenly. "I'm too big for her to hold my hand."

Then Mother, Jean still in her arms, pushed through the growing crowd and knelt by Emily.

"She's okay," Emily said. Her voice croaked oddly.

I sound like Mrs. Thurstone, she thought in surprise.

Jean's face was buried in her aunt's neck. Emily reached out to her.

"Ann's all right, Jean," she comforted the small girl. "She's not dead at all."

"Did she think I was DEAD!" Ann exclaimed, her eyes enormous.

At the sound of her sister's voice, Jean's back stiffened. Still she did not turn her head. She was afraid to believe.

"She had the breath knocked out of her at first," the young man explained. He too sounded like Mrs. Thurstone, Emily noticed. "I wondered if she was dead myself till I got to her . . ."

Jean twisted around and looked at Ann.

"You're not killed?" she said, making sure.

"I almost was," Ann decided, liking the attention. "You should have held my hand."

"We'd better take her up to Emergency, just in case," the young man said to Elizabeth Blair. "I'll gladly drive you if you haven't a car. I'd like to be sure she's okay myself. I didn't see her till she'd run into me. Thank God I wasn't going fast!"

Suddenly, belatedly, Ann burst into tears.

"I got hit by a car!" she wailed. "And I hurt myself!"

Jean wrenched free from her aunt's grasp and ran away from all of them, back to the house. Mrs. Blair gathered Ann up gently and spoke to her daughter.

"I'm going to take her up to the hospital, Emily," she explained carefully. "You'll have to look after things at home. You'll have to convince Jean, somehow, that this is not her fault. She's too little to be responsible."

Emily rose. She looked at Ann, now crying quietly, her head on her aunt's shoulder. Then she went to the house.

She found Jean, face down, under her bed. The older girl sat down and peered in at the miserable bundle of humanity with its back to her.

"Jean, Ann's all right," she said, hoping she was telling the truth.

"I tried to make her hold my hand. But I couldn't. She ran out. It is so my fault!" Jean sobbed.

"No," Emily said. She was face to face with it now. "I knew you were too little, and I should never have let you go without me. You tried your best."

Jean, dusty and tear-streaked, crawled out.

"Was it really your fault, Emily?" She wanted to be sure.

Emily nodded, but it was the unhappiness in her eyes that convinced the four-year-old.

"Don't feel so bad," Jean comforted, putting both arms around Emily's neck and hugging her. "Ann's fine."

"Of course she is," Emily said steadily, keeping her fears to herself. "How would you like to help me start getting supper ready?"

They went down the stairs, hand in hand. As they reached the hall, the boys came charging in.

"Emily, a girl was here wanting you," John started. "She said she'd come back. Where's Ann?"

Jean burst out with the story.

Kate came, Emily thought. Then, seeing terror on the boy's faces, she pushed Kate Bloomfield out of her mind and hurried to set Jean's facts straight.

"She wasn't really run over, and she wasn't all bloody, Jean. What on earth are you saying?"

"Where is she then?" John asked.

"Mother took her to the hospital—just to check and be sure." Emily hurried the words and did not meet his stern young eyes. "But she's fine!"

James ran off to watch television. Jean tugged at Emily's hand.

"Come ON, Emily. You said we'd get supper."

But John had not stirred. Emily waited.

"Sometimes when people get hit like that, Emily," the boy said slowly, "they get hurt inside and nobody knows."

Emily looked quickly at Jean, but she was not really listening. John, too, glanced at his little sister and was quiet.

He and Emily eyed each other, both needing to share their worry, yet neither wanting to hear it expressed and made more real.

"I'll go out front and wait," he said.

He ran. Emily wanted to go with him and keep watch for the car bringing Ann home again.

"Come ON, Emily," Jean said again.

Wilhelmina Shakespeare met them at the kitchen door. She wove around their legs, crying piteously.

"She's hungry," Jean said, stooping to pat her. "She wants Sophie."

So do I, Emily thought.

"Where is she anyway?" she asked.

"At Mrs. Thurstone's."

Emily remembered Mrs. Thurstone's sprained wrist and sighed. That meant Sophie would be away till they were ready to eat.

"Hello, I am here!" a voice cried from the doorway.

"Sophie!" Jean shouted.

Emily was too old to hurl herself at Sophie the way Jean did, but welcome shone in her startled face. How had Sophie guessed?

"Mrs. Thurstone . . . she saw your mother going away in a car from her window," Sophie explained, her English still sounding very French. "So she tells me 'Sophie, go and find out what is the matter—and do not come back until all is well.' But I will not go before I get her in her bed. So now I am here."

Five minutes later, she had the story from them. While she listened, clucking with sympathy, she also fed Willie, started Jean setting the table and set Emily to making a salad. Emily still listened for the sound of a car in the driveway, but slicing tomatoes and chopping lettuce made waiting easier.

"They're here!" John yelled.

Emily knew, by his voice, that everything was all right, but she could not seem to move. Suppose she was wrong. Suppose Ann . . .

"Go now, Emily," Sophie said, taking the paring knife from her and giving her a gentle push.

Mother was looking for her over the heads of the other children.

"Here she is, Emily," she said, putting Ann down on her own two feet, "all in one piece. Maybe even wiser."

Sophie broke the tension.

"Supper is ready," she said, her voice sounding wonderfully as usual.

"Oh, Sophie!" said Mrs. Blair, and the look in her eyes was exactly the look of thanksgiving that had been in her daughter's minutes before. "Is Peter home? No, of course not. He had to work late. Come on, children. Are your hands clean?"

Emily watched Ann as she ran to wash her hands and then came trotting back to climb up on her chair. She looked so terribly ordinary—and so terribly special.

She's fine, Emily thought, loving Ann so much she was afraid she would cry. Instead, she sat down hastily and bowed her head for the blessing. Not once did she think of Kate Bloomfield or of the box still waiting upstairs on her bed.

11

Kate Lends a Hand

Emily was up to her ears in children when the doorbell rang. Her mother, on her way out the door to a meeting, called up, "It's someone for you, Emily. I'm sending her on up."

"Oh, split peas and applesauce!" Emily said. "It must be Kate."

Emily was sitting on Jean's bed trying to get the knot out of Ann's shoelace. Jean, who was undressing herself, had just become stuck in her dress. She had it pulled up over her head and both her arms free, but she could not get her face out, and she was calling for help and staggering blindly around the room searching for her cousin.

James and John, who should have been in the bathtub by now, were in the hall. John was building something secret and mysterious with a collection of old boxes and some tape, and had not even started to undress. James had taken off all his clothes but a pair of underpants and had tied one end of his big towel around his throat. He was tearing up and down so that it would float out behind him like a Superman cape, and he was yelling and banging his chest like Tarzan.

Emily dropped Ann's foot, grabbed at Jean, called to James to stop "this instant"—and Kate was there.

"I have the box ready," Emily told Kate, trying to free Jean while she spoke.

But Kate seemed to have forgotten why she had come. She stood, half in the hall, half in the doorway to the girls' bedroom, and stared.

"Emily," Jean called, still lost in the dress and beginning to get frightened. "Get me OUT!"

Ann slid down from the bed and shoved at her sister.

"She's undoing my shoe first," she shouted, so that Jean would be sure to hear.

"Emily, can I use your Magic Marker?" John's voice reached them.

"No, because you're going to get undressed," Emily said firmly. "Don't push her, Annie. All right, Jean! Why didn't you undo it at the neck first?"

"But my shoe—" Ann began. "Can that girl untie shoes?"

"Oh dear . . ." Emily reddened. "Why can't you just WAIT! I'm sorry, Kate," she apologized.

"I'll try to get it undone," Kate offered.

She sat down and began working at the knot. Emily, all at once feeling as lighthearted as a singing bird, pulled Jean's dress back on, undid the fastening, and slid the dress off easily. She started the girls' bath water. She went out and herded John and James up the stairs to their bath. She paused to admire John's building, in passing, and had to get down on her hands and knees to see the secret passage he had made. James was still being Super-Tarzan when he reached the bathroom. While Emily had her back turned for an instant, he stood up on the end of the tub and "flew" into the waiting water. He banged his head and elbow, bellowed with rage, and sent half the bath water cascading out of the tub. At last Emily left them, hoping for the best but knowing it was unlikely, and raced down to see what stage the girls had reached. Kate had them both in the tub. They were chattering away with her as though they had known each other for years.

"I can do them," Emily offered, going to take over. There was a crash from the floor above.

"I'll finish here," Kate said quickly, holding on to the washcloth. "You go back to the others. This is fun."

Emily turned and met a dripping James.

"John punched me," he told her, "and he won't give me any room."

"And what did you do to John?" Emily asked, shooing him back.

"I was being a dolphin," James explained, "and they always leap, Emily. Remember the ones we saw on TV?"

"Did you leap on top of him?"

"Sort of . . . but it was an accident . . . and he hit me ON PURPOSE!"

They reached the bathroom. John was operating a submarine fleet.

"Hey, James, you be one of the captains and we'll talk on the radio," he invited.

Joyfully, the dolphin leapt back into the tub. One of his feet flattened the periscope on John's best submarine. The battle raged again.

"Quit that!" Emily yelled at them, whacking whichever boy was nearest. "If you're not done in five minutes, no story!"

Twenty minutes later, when the three of them went down to the girls' room, Kate had already read one book. The girls' clothes hung neatly on the backs of chairs. Emily sighed admiringly. The rooms upstairs looked as though a hurricane had swept through them.

"Now, boys," said Jean primly, "keep quiet and let Kate read. Make James sit on the floor, Emily. He pushes."

Insulted, James immediately fought for room on the bed. John, laughing, tried to drag him to the floor. Ann kicked at both of them when they came near her. Jean prepared to burst into tears.

Kate's mouth dropped open in amazement at the uproar, but Emily, after two months, was used to it. She separated the boys. Then she made the girls move over so that James and John could sit one on either side of Kate.

"But, Emily, we were good!" Jean protested.

"So were the boys," lied Emily.

"Don't forget I was nearly dead," Ann remarked.

Emily ignored her. "Read, Kate, read," she urged.

"'Once there was a little doll who lived in a pocket,'" Kate began.

Impunity Jane was really too long to start this late, but Emily loved it as much as the children did, and she could tell that Kate was discovering it for the first time. She settled down contentedly to listen. Soon, Ann slid off the bed and came to curl up on her lap. Emily looked down at the scraped cheek and held the small girl close.

"'As for the doll's house, it was given away. As for the bead cushion, it was lost,'" Kate finished.

"Good," Jean said through a huge yawn. She crawled over John and got under her covers. Emily stood up carefully and carried Ann, who had fallen fast asleep, across the room to her bed. Kate came too, without being asked, and turned down the bedclothes.

"Okay, boys," Emily said, turning.

They were wrestling in the hall.

"Goodness!" Kate said.

But Emily simply pulled them apart once again and escorted them every step of the way to their beds. Then she ran to her room and snatched up the box she had wondered about for so long, and hurried down to where Kate waited.

Kate stood looking at it for a moment. Then she turned it over in her hands, examining it.

"You really didn't get it open, did you?" she said, grinning at Emily.

"Of course I didn't," Emily retorted. She took care not to think of hatchets. "How could I? What's so special about it anyway—and how come it was in my room?"

Kate opened her mouth and closed it again.

"I can't tell you right now," she said. "I would if I could. I have to go home now. Maybe . . ."

Maybe what? Emily longed to shout at her.

But she could wait a while longer. She had her own ideas about that box. Kate was going to tell. She was sure of that.

"Thanks for helping with the kids," she said gruffly, following Kate to the door.

Kate turned back for an instant, her face shining.

"It was wonderful," she said.

The door closed behind her. Emily was alone. The box was gone.

12

The Secret

Emily slid the note down onto her lap and opened it.

EMILY BLAIR
GO DOWN INTO YOUR CELLAR AT
FOUR THIRTY THIS AFTERNOON.
BRING NOBODY WITH YOU.
DO NOT TURN ON A LIGHT.
BE THERE WITHOUT FAIL!
YOU WILL BE TOLD ALL!!!

She read it through twice. Then she scrunched up the scrap of paper and shoved it into her desk.

Kate was too far away to have tossed the note at her, but Emily looked across at her anyway. Kate was extremely busy copying down an assignment from the board, but her mouth quirked up as Emily watched.

They're going to tell me today, Emily exulted.

Lindsay Ross was also very busy. She bent over a textbook and read intently. But her back had a knowing look.

Emily shook with laughter. Mr. Adamson looked in her direction. She, too, snatched up her pencil and became a model student.

If only she could get away from John, James, Jean, and Ann! she worried as the day inched by. She hurried home, prepared to beg her mother to keep the children out of her way. But there was no need. She found Jean and Ann "helping" Sophie make cookies and the boys out playing with school friends.

It was time! Emily opened the cellar door and peered down into total darkness. Swallowing, she lowered one foot onto the first step. It creaked eerily, like a stairway in a haunted house. Emily paused. She still meant to go down. Of course she did. But a prickle of terror went up her back.

Willie appeared from nowhere and saved her. Meowing in a worried way, the cat went ahead of Emily into the deep shadow.

"You're 'nobody,' aren't you, cat?" Emily said, and followed her.

Her heart was thumping like a bongo drum when she reached the bottom. Uncertain what was expected of her, she stopped there and stood, waiting.

"Is that youuuuuuu, Emily Blair?" a ghostly voice asked.

"Yes," quavered Emily, half laughing, half scared-to-death.

Then Kate turned on a flashlight. She and Lindsay were sitting on a couple of cartons, grinning.

"It's just us," Kate said unnecessarily. "We had a club—"

"And you used to meet in this house!" Emily finished.

She had been right all along.

"I told you she'd guess, Lin," Kate said. "Seeing the box and everything."

Lindsay nodded. "But you didn't know who passed you the note, did you?" she said.

"Not for sure," Emily answered. She had been almost positive, but if Lindsay wanted to think she had been so mysterious, Emily would not spoil it.

"You didn't even turn your head," Emily added, going all the way.

"I'm sneaky," Lindsay bragged.

They showed her the cellar window minus a pane, through which they had got into the house. It was behind a bush. Her father must have overlooked it.

"There used to be lots of places," Kate said, a touch of sadness in her voice.

"Come on up to my room," Emily offered quickly. "It's cold down here and spooky."

The three of them trooped up to the attic. As they passed room after room, Lindsay could not get over how different they looked. Kate had been there the night before but, now that she was not surrounded by Sutherlands, she too was astonished at the way a haunted house had become a home.

When they emerged from the cellar, Emily got a surprise of her own, but she said nothing about it. Until then she had seen Kate only in school clothes. Now she had on faded jeans, a sloppy sweatshirt worn backwards with CAMP WONDERWAYS printed across it, and sneakers without socks. Her short hair needed combing. She held the box under her arm.

They reached Emily's bedroom door. She pushed it open and stepped back. The shock on their faces was all she could have wished for.

She remembered the room as she had first seen it, as they must have left it in June. Grey, streaked walls. Grimy woodwork. Dusty windows. Now both the casement window and the skylight sparkled. The walls were the soft yellow Emily herself had chosen. The woodwork was a gleaming white. The brown floor had been covered with green tiles and a bright braided rug. And Emily's furniture was just right.

"I don't believe it," Kate said finally.

Emily led the way in. As she turned to close

the door, shutting out all interruptions, Wilhelmina Shakespeare stalked through it.

"I *thought* I heard a cat in the cellar," Lindsay said. "Emily, how do you rate a room like this and a cat too?"

"And four brothers and sisters," added Kate.

"They aren't my brothers and sisters," Emily explained, "and Willie's really Sophie's cat."

They settled down to talk then, Emily and Lindsay on the bed, Kate collapsed in comfort on the floor. Emily went on to tell them the story of the "impossible summer."

"There we were, three of us with NO PETS ALLOWED," she summed it up, "and now here we are with the four kids and Uncle Roger, when he has time off, and Daisy and Willie and Sophie—and Willie's kittens any day!"

She took them to inspect Daisy. The gerbil was asleep, nose to tail, and refused to show off.

"My sister Laurel had a hamster when I was small," Lindsay said as they returned to their places. Emily thought of explaining she had met Laurel, but there was really nothing to tell.

"She wants to be a nurse and work with mentally retarded children," Lindsay said. She hesitated. "I think it's because of James, my brother. I mean, I *know* it's because of James. He's retarded. He's fifteen now. He's in high school."

Startled, Emily thought of James Ross. He had been tall. His ears had stuck out, she remembered. He had not seemed different. But he had seemed younger than fifteen.

"I'm sort of an afterthought," Lindsay continued, unaware of Emily's thoughts.

She laughed at what she herself had said and added, "Not really, I guess. Laurel says I'm Mama's pet—and she's right. Sometimes I wish Mama would pick somebody else to be her pet. I get tired of being perfect all the time!"

"Like heck you do!" Kate jeered. She was lying full-length on the floor now, propped up on her elbow. She scowled at Lindsay's account of her family.

"I really was an afterthought," she said savagely. "And they didn't want me one bit. My sister Marilyn told me so. Sometimes I think they still don't."

"Oh, Kate, they do too," Lindsay soothed.

"Well, they're stuck with me anyway," Kate conceded, flattening out and reaching a hand to stroke Wilhelmina Shakespeare. Willie muttered and dodged away from her.

"She never acts like that," Emily said in surprise as the cat sought the darkest corner of the room. But Kate was still thinking of her parents.

"I don't see much of them, and they don't see much of me. Okay, Lin. Forget it."

Emily wanted to know more, though, and she asked questions until she had Kate's family straight in her mind too. Kate's only sister was married and had a baby boy.

"You're an aunt," Emily said, impressed.

"Sure am. Aunt Kate," Kate agreed. "I've never seen him," she explained, seeing Emily was puzzled by her indifference. "They moved to Calgary after they got married. David's a doctor, and it's hard for Mother and Dad to leave the store. They've started talking, though, about going out there at Christmas. Dad says Christmas is the very worst time to leave the store—but Mother really wants to go. We're going to fly."

"What kind of store?" Emily asked.

"Great Caesar's ghost, you mean you have never heard of BLOOMFIELD'S BOOKS?" Kate looked at Emily as though she had said the world was flat.

"A bookstore! Really?" Emily was excited at once.

Kate groaned, but Emily could see the pride behind her scorn.

"They started it after Marilyn went to school and before I was born. It's all paperbacks. Both of them work there, and it stays open most nights because lots of people come then to browse," Kate filled in the picture. "That's what I mean about being an afterthought. When I arrived, I nearly wrecked the book business. Mother got somebody to take care of me, though, and went back to the store as soon as she could. They eat, drink, talk, and sleep books!"

Kate was silent. Emily, not looking at her, thought, It sounds lonely.

Then she thought of something else she wanted explained. Kate, catching her hesitating, said, "Let's hear it, whatever it is."

"What did you mean when you said you were incorrigible?" Emily asked.

Kate shouted with laughter.

"Mother wants me to be a lady. She hates me wearing old clothes and acting like a boy. But I wish I were a boy. Sometimes I do, anyway. Boys can go out and do things," she said wistfully. "I give my mother a hard time," she boasted swiftly, covering up.

Lindsay sniffed. "Well, I wish you wouldn't," she said. "I know you're not really like that, but Mama says 'What do you want to go around with that wild Kate Bloomfield for?' She should see the stuff you—"

Kate silenced her with one look. Both of them turned and stared at Emily. Their eyes searched her face. The girl sat still and endured it. She knew the time had almost come. They were about to tell ALL.

"Our club—" Kate began. She stopped.

"Kate, we have to tell her," Lindsay said reasonably. Emily noted with interest that what Kate said went, as far as this club was concerned. "We can't tell what she'll think without letting her know."

Kate sat up straight and studied her sneakers. Nobody said anything. Emily went on waiting. Then both girls spoke at once, their sentences colliding.

"It's a Writing Club," Lindsay said defiantly.

"We write poems," Kate confessed, glaring at Emily.

Emily's heart leapt with joy and relief.

"So do I," she told them, laughing at the disbelief and then the happiness on their faces. "I have for years. No kidding!"

"I should have guessed," Kate said at last, "with a cat named Wilhelmina Shakespeare."

13

"To Friends"

The key hung on a string around Kate's neck.

"I might have known," Emily said, remembering the hours she had spent searching for it. She pointed to the dire warnings pasted on the lid of the box. "Beware of what beast?"

"Me," Kate snarled, baring her teeth.

As the others laughed, she unlocked the box. Then she lifted the lid. Emily craned her neck. At last! At long last! But Kate let it drop shut again.

"You're probably wondering why we kept our poems here," she said.

"No, not really." Emily was too impatient to be polite. Kate did not notice. She was concentrating on looping the string with the key on it around and around her right wrist.

"My mother and father always pull apart things they read," she explained. "Things that sound fine to me! If I showed them what I wrote, I know they'd be polite . . . but they'd see all the wrong things underneath. I've heard them laugh at other people's poems."

Emily thought of that one poem of Kate's she had read. Bits of it still sang in her memory.

. . . And my feet got up dancing . . .

She did not know the Bloomfields, of course. Still . . .

"I don't think they'd laugh," she said impulsively.

Kate's dark eyes flashed up at her with a question in them. Emily sounded so sure. But Lindsay heard nothing odd in the words.

"Mine love what I write," she assured Kate. Kate was now weaving the string in and out between her fingers. Watching her, Emily guessed that Kate's poems and Lindsay's were very different. Perhaps their parents were different too.

"At least, Mama really likes them." Lindsay turned to Emily. "My father doesn't like any poetry. He says if you have something to say, why not just say it without rhyming and fancy words."

"Mine gave me books of poems before I could

even read." Kate's voice sounded loud in the small room.

Emily thought of her own father with quick love. He liked her poems, all that she showed him. She could not remember having seen him read other poetry to himself, but he snatched any chance to recite those he had learned as "memory work" in school when he was a boy. Emily had grown up with "Invictus," "If," and a score of others. She had come to know bits of them by heart, over the years. Sometimes at night, before she slept, she would say lines she loved over to herself.

This be the verse you grave for me:
Here he lies where he longed to be;
Home is the sailor, home from sea,
And the hunter home from the hill.

and

Loveliest of trees, the cherry now
Is hung with bloom along the bough.

She knew all of that one. She had heard it every spring of her life. He knew funny ones too, like "Father William." And wonderful long ones like "The Highwayman" and "The Lady of Shalott."

Did Kate's parents laugh at poems like that?

"What does Laurel say about yours?" she asked Lindsay, struggling to get on safer ground.

"She says she's seen worse—but not much

worse!" Lindsay made a face, but Emily could tell that she was not really angry. "Laurel thinks she's so smart sometimes," she added.

Kate reached to open the box again. Suddenly rain spattered on the skylight. All three of them looked up.

"It's dark in here." Emily turned on the lamp beside her bed.

Come on, rain! she wished, knowing what happened inside her room when it stormed. Yet maybe the others would not see it. Maybe it was only special to her.

The storm arrived as if it had heard her. Rain drummed on the roof, rattled against the glass. Wind blew around the eaves and fought to get in at them through the tightly closed casement window. In the heart of it all, the small, slant-roofed room glowed, snug and safe.

"It's like being in a ship out on the ocean!" Kate had to shout above the din, but Emily saw the delight in her face.

"What time is it?" Lindsay, too, shouted. Her voice broke the spell. Emily moved till she could see her clock.

"Nearly six."

"Oh, am I in big trouble!" Lindsay shot off the bed and headed for the door. "We're going out for dinner. And I don't have a raincoat!"

"Mother will give her an umbrella," said Emily. She did not move, still hoping to see inside the box. But it was no use.

"I should go too." Kate stood up, tucking the box back under her arm.

Feeling like a pricked balloon, Emily got to her feet. Then she caught sight of Wilhelmina Shakespeare, hunched up in the corner of the room, her fur on end, her eyes round and wild.

"It's all right, Willie. Just some rain," she said, going to get her. "It's time to have your supper."

The cat gave her one unseeing look, made a harsh noise deep in her throat, and streaked away through the door.

Emily straightened and stared after her.

"Maybe it's the kittens coming. She doesn't usually mind storms—and she likes being picked up."

They were at the bottom of the attic stairs before Kate murmured, "I'd love a kitten."

"Well, when she does have them—" Emily began.

"I can't have one." Kate thrust rejection at Emily like a shield. All at once she was the girl she had been the night they met. Her lips bit tightly together. Her eyes were cold. Emily did not finish her sentence or ask any questions. The two of them went the rest of the way down without speaking.

Mrs. Blair met them in the hall.

"You must be Kate," she said, holding out her hand.

Emily fumed. Why, why did her parents always insist on shaking hands with people?

Nobody else in the entire world did, she was certain. She waited for Kate to fumble and be embarrassed. But Kate Bloomfield was more of a lady than her mother suspected. The tough, see-if-I-care Kate vanished. The Kate who wrote poems shook hands easily and smiled at Emily's mother.

You'd think she had on her best clothes, Emily marveled, seeing the sweatshirt, the jeans, and the sneakers through her mother's eyes.

"I'm sorry I was in such a hurry when I let you in last night," Elizabeth Blair apologized.

"That's okay."

With that, Kate's poise disappeared. It should be simple to say good-bye to these friendly people and leave. It was not simple. All Kate could think of was "I gotta go now." That sounded so wrong she could not bring herself to say it. She looked at the floor and juggled the box nervously in her hands.

If only the Blairs would do something, say something.

The two of them stood politely, waiting for her to go.

"It's KATE!"

"Kate! Kate!"

Jean and Ann, on their way to the dining room, had spotted her. They ran to her as though she were a lifelong friend of theirs, a friend they had not seen for months.

Kate bent to hug them. An instant before, she had been plain and ill at ease. Now she sparkled.

"Careful of the box," she warned Ann.

She doesn't look lonely, Emily thought.

She scoffed at her own thought the next instant. What in the world had made her think Kate looked especially alone?

"Kate," Mrs. Blair said, "would your mother let you stay for supper?"

Emily barely managed to keep her astonishment from showing. Mother had often let her have guests to meals, but this was the first time she had invited one of Emily's friends without Emily asking her first. She studied her mother's face. Elizabeth Blair did not glance at her daughter. She was waiting for Kate's answer.

Kate did not hesitate. "Oh, she won't mind. She's working late. She told me to heat up a TV dinner."

Mrs. Blair did not appear to see anything strange in Kate's words, but Emily could feel her own eyes widen.

"Wonderful. Set an extra place, Emily. We're just ready. Girls, let Kate go so she can walk."

Emily bent her head over the cutlery drawer, getting out a knife, fork, and spoon.

"I want to sit by Kate," both little girls demanded as she started to arrange the utensils.

"She's *my* friend," Emily told them.

It was too late to catch the words back. Her cheeks flamed. She had only known Kate for two days. Kate probably did not think of her as a friend at all. Not yet. Why had she said that? If only she'd taken time to think!

"All RIGHT!" she snapped, giving in and moving Kate's place to between the children. She still did not look up at the other girl.

"*Madame*, I cannot find Willie to give her her food," Sophie said from the kitchen door.

"She came downstairs ahead of us," Emily said indifferently.

"Sophie, how's Mrs. Thurstone?" Mrs. Blair stopped the girl to ask.

"She is in her bed with supper on a tray," Sophie said.

"But there's no light over there!"

"She can see out better when the light is off," Sophie reminded her.

Elizabeth Blair laughed and looked over at the dark house.

"I should wave to her," she said.

"Just don't pull the drapes," Emily told her.

She looked at Kate then and caught bewilderment on her face. Relaxing, Emily explained about the old lady next door who liked to keep an eye on the Blairs. Kate grinned. The rest of the family gathered.

Elizabeth Blair looked around, counting.

"Let's see your hands, James. Not bad! Sophie," she called, "leave Willie till later. Everyone's here but you."

"Lasagna," Emily said. "Yum, yum!"

She pushed Ann's chair in and sat down herself.

Then Sophie exploded into the dining room.

"Ils naissent, je crois—les petits chats! Ils naissent—dans la boîte à bois."

Everyone stared at her. Then Mother jumped to her feet.

"The kittens!" she flung at the rest of them. "In the woodbox, I think. Oh, don't tell us, Sophie. Show us!"

Leaving the lasagna to get cold, they flocked out of the dining room.

"Hush, hush," Mother quieted them as they jammed into an excited knot at the living-room door. "We mustn't disturb her. No, John, turn that light down again. Now go gently . . ."

Even James and John walked on tiptoe. Willie was in the box which held wood for the fireplace when Dad remembered to fill it. The family grouped around her, standing far enough back not to crowd her but near enough to be part of the miracle that was happening. Willie might have been waiting for them to arrive. The moment they were all there she heaved, gave a brief cry—and, in a matter of minutes, there, in the box, was her first kitten.

"What's that?" Ann squeaked.

"You watch," Mother said, pulling her niece close to her.

The cat raised her head and licked at the small, wet bundle. It was in a sac.

"They come in packages," James said, "like Saran Wrap."

The membrane broke. Willie cleaned it away. The tiny kitten, eyes shut tight, ears flat, legs too weak to hold it up, squirmed helplessly. Its mother nudged it firmly until it nuzzled against her.

Wilhelmina ignored it after that. Certain it was safe and sound, she was busy having another one.

The first kitten was black, the second striped like its mother. Wilhelmina was licking it with her rasping tongue when the doorbell rang. The cat was the only one who did not jump at the jangle of sound.

"I go." Sophie, on her knees by the woodbox, started up.

"No, you stay with Willie." Mrs. Blair looked annoyed. "Who on earth would come right at suppertime? Emily, you answer it."

Kate came along, without waiting to be asked. Before they could get there, however, the bell sounded again, abrupt and angry.

"Maybe I'd better get it." Dad caught up with them. "Someone sounds violent."

He pulled the door open with a jerk, and found himself faced with a very cross Mrs. Thurstone.

"Mrs. Thurstone," Mother gasped from the living-room doorway, "what is it? What's wrong?"

"What's wrong indeed," the old lady croaked, tapping into the hall, looking like a ruffled little old hen. "There I am in my bed, eating my supper as any sensible person should be—and I happen to glance out my window . . ."

The Blairs were careful not to look at one another.

"One minute, you're all sitting down to supper. The next, without touching your victuals, you're up and into the parlor! I want to know what's going on. Don't you laugh at me, young man," she finished, her voice rising.

Dad swallowed his grin in a hurry, but Mother went off into a peal of delighted laughter.

"Good for you, Mrs. Thurstone," she said warmly, putting her arm around the old woman's shoulders ("as though she wasn't a witch at all" Jean said later). "Come and I'll show you."

Another kitten had been born while they were away. It was black with white feet.

"I think that is all," Sophie told them.

Wilhelmina Shakespeare seemed to think that was plenty. She lay back and rested, her green eyes closed. The last little kitten had only had a lick and a promise.

Mrs. Thurstone peered down at the tired cat and the three new kittens. A small, almost shy, smile warmed her craggy old face.

"Well," she said, "kittens! I had visions of broken legs or heart attacks. Kittens never crossed my mind. I pulled on my old coat over my nightclothes and came any old whichway. No fool like an old fool! That's what my mother used to say."

"Did you have a mother?" Jean asked, her eyes wide.

"Gracious, child, did you think I dropped from heaven?" the old lady said testily.

"I thought you flew on a broomstick," Jean began.

Hastily, Mother interrupted.

"I have an idea," she cried. "Let's have a party. For once, we'll have dessert first. The lasagna must be cold anyway. Sit here, Mrs. Thurstone."

She lowered the guest gently into a chair.

"Such carryings on!" the old lady muttered, but she did not offer to leave. Her black eyes were as bright as Ann's.

"A christening party for the kittens!" Peter Blair caught his wife's mood. "Hamlet, Ophelia, and Richard the Third, I suppose?"

"I think we should name one Superman." James sat cross-legged near the box, watching the new members of the family.

"I had a cat once called Mr. Atkins," Mrs. Thurstone told them suddenly.

"Mr. Atkins !" the children echoed.

"He looked like a man who lived up the street from us. Sly!"

"She's really something, isn't she?" Kate bent close to Emily to whisper.

Emily nodded very slightly. She did not believe in witches, of course, but she felt sure it was not safe to say anything you did not want Mrs. Thurstone to hear.

Elizabeth and Peter Blair returned with food and drink. Mother gave everyone a glass of ginger ale.

"Now let's make some toasts," she said, sitting on the arm of Mrs. Thurstone's chair. "What shall we drink to?"

"To Wilhelmina Shakespeare and her children!" John raised his glass with a flourish, proud that he knew just how to do it.

Everyone drank to Willie and the kittens.

"James?" Dad invited.

James held his glass high, thought hard, and then, his eyes twinkling, said, "To firemen!"

"Dopey, we could have got down without them," John scoffed.

Peter Blair shifted, stretching around the little girls on his lap.

"To Roger and to Deborah, who are with us, even though they're not here," he said quietly, reaching his glass and sipping from it.

Nobody said anything for a moment. Emily saw John swallow and knew he was wanting his mother and father so much it hurt.

"*Santé!*" cried Sophie, distracting him. He looked at her, interest kindling in his face.

"What did she say?" he asked.

"Good health!" Mrs. Thurstone translated.

Mother turned her head and smiled with a sudden, special sweetness at the old lady sitting so erectly next to her. She laid her free hand gently over the bandage on Mrs. Thurstone's wrist.

"To good neighbors," she said softly.

The old woman looked down at that hand,

cleared her throat, and corrected her loudly and clearly in her cracked voice. "To friends!"

"Hold up your glass, Jean." Dad started to show her.

"I know how," the little girl told him haughtily. She raised her tumbler higher than anyone. "To parties!" she said, as though she had been making toasts all her life.

"To parties," Ann copied her.

"That's MY toast!"

"All right, Jeanie. It's such a good one two people can make it," Dad told her. He looked across at the older girls.

"How about Emily?"

"Kate first." Emily had no words ready.

"Mine's the same as Mrs. Thurstone's," Kate said. She took a big gulp of her ginger ale and choked, but Emily saw her looking at her over the glass.

What had Mrs. Thurstone said? Emily thought she knew, but she had to be sure. Kate's eyes were waiting. Then Emily was sure. Her face lighted with joy.

"That's mine too," she said. Then, growing brave in her new happiness, she spoke the words aloud for them both to hear.

"To friends!" said Emily Blair.

This time, she did not wish the word unsaid. This time, it sang with rightness.

14

The Quill Club

But I still haven't read their poems, Emily thought when Kate had gone home. And they haven't read mine!

Lindsay had an appointment with the orthodontist the next afternoon. On Thursday she had a music lesson. On Friday she had to go straight home because Laurel was there overnight and Mrs. Ross wanted the family together.

"Don't you two *dare* go ahead without me!" she ordered Kate and Emily.

Lindsay was used to having her own way. Emily and Kate promised.

Then it was Saturday! Glorious, free Saturday, the dream day of the week, the day Emily regarded as her own personal property. Wakening, she smiled. This morning, finally, the Club would meet. Nothing could go wrong, nothing.

But five things did go wrong. The first was rain, a steady, grey, all-day rain. The other four were John, James, Jean, and Ann.

"Mother," Emily begged, "Kate and Lindsay are coming over. Can't you keep the kids away?"

"Emily Ann, the television is broken," Mrs. Blair announced. It was as though she said "The sky has fallen."

"But couldn't you—"

"Sophie and I have already begun making a batch of pickles. And I must go over and see how Mrs. Thurstone is. Perhaps the children will amuse themselves."

Emily made a hideous face.

"With Kate here? Fat chance!"

"Yes, they do love Kate," Mother agreed. "But haven't you seen how much fun she has with them?"

Emily had seen. Kate now spent more time at the Blairs' than she did at home. Mother had grown worried about what Mrs. Bloomfield would think of Kate's coming across the street every afternoon, staying to supper three nights in a row, and not getting home before eight o'clock. She had phoned to explain. Emily had heard her and Dad talking about the conversation afterwards.

"You'd almost think Kate was a dog somebody

had given them that they didn't know what to do with," she said indignantly. "No wonder the child's always underfoot, Peter! She's hungry for a home."

"Now, Elizabeth." Dad tried to cool her anger. "It's not like you to jump to conclusions. Somebody's made Kate the fine girl she is—and her parents are the most likely candidates."

"If you could have heard her mother! She sounded indifferent!"

"She was probably just tired. It can't be easy, working in that store all day. Kate does seem hungry for something we have here, but I suspect it's brothers and sisters. She *has* a home, Elizabeth."

"Not what I call a home!" Mother retorted, still upset by the lack of concern in Kate's mother's voice.

Emily's heart had wrenched with sorrow for Kate. So she was right about her parents! They really did not want her.

Then Elizabeth Blair about-faced.

"Maybe you're right. I haven't even met the woman, after all. And I've never seen a girl who cares more for little children than Kate."

It was one thing to like helping to put children to bed or sitting next to them at supper, Emily thought gloomily. What would Kate feel when she learned that, on Saturday mornings, there was no way to get rid of them?

And Lindsay! She had not encountered the

Sutherlands yet. But Emily was certain that Lindsay would not welcome a morning of children any more than Kate.

Emily grew cunning. She gave John her colored pencils and a pad of notepaper so he could draw battleships and spacemen. She reminded James of the kittens, and went with him to see them. They were so small and sweet that she nearly stayed to watch them too. Just in time, she remembered her mission. She found things to offer James later—an old peaked cap, a plastic canteen. Maybe she could get him started playing explorers. Both boys would like that.

She went in search of Jean and Ann.

"We're playing hospital," Jean said at once.

"Teddy's head is off again. He had a dreadful accident." Ann held up her battered bear in two pieces. "Maybe somebody should have been holding his hand," she added slyly.

Jean's lips quivered.

"But the doctors can fix him with lots of bandages and three operations," her little sister relented.

Emily hurried away, rejoicing. Maybe she and Lindsay and Kate would be undisturbed after all.

They had half an hour. They all sat on Emily's bed to share their poems. It was terrible and wonderful too, reading your own words to someone who might not understand—and yet just might.

Lindsay's poetry was dreadful.

I like flowers because they are pretty.
They grow in the country as well as the city.
Their leaves are green and they are
    different hues.
Red, yellow, blue, pink.
I don't know which I like best to choose.

Lindsay read the words aloud. Emily could
see that she was pleased with them, proud of
having made them rhyme. But they were not like
Emily's words, part of herself put on paper.
Lindsay grinned at the uncertainty on Emily's
face.

"I like them," she said with no resentment.
"You look just like Laurel when I read them to
her. I'll bet you'll like Kate's better. But I think
mine are nicer. Most of Kate's are mad, and lots
don't even rhyme."

It was hard for Kate to start. When she did,
gruffly, hiding behind her paper, Emily could
see why.

I come in.
Nobody asks "Where have you been?"
They do not care
If I am there.
They have had a "hard day."
They never say
"What about you?

Are you tired out too?"
If, someday, they ask me "Are you well?"
I will not tell.

Emily reached out and touched Kate's foot. She
did not know what to say. Kate used words the
way she herself did except that they jarred more.
Kate's words were Kate. Emily's words were Emily.
And, she supposed, looking at Lindsay's pretty
face, Lindsay's words might even be Lindsay.

"Read one of yours now," the other two told her.

Emily cleared her throat and ducked behind
the paper as Kate had done.

It's suppertime.
The grace is sung.
And over walls and cloth so white,
Tall candles shed their light.

It's suppertime.
The silver gleams.
The crimson rosebuds shyly hide
Their hearts from us outside.

It's suppertime.
The laughter grows.
My mother smiles, a lovely sight.
God shares our meal tonight.

"That's beautiful," Lindsay said promptly.
"Better than mine."

Emily, still caught up in the picture she had made, came back to the others slowly. Kate said nothing at all. Emily waited.

"That is the way it really is here," Kate told her at last.

Emily laughed, freed suddenly from a fear that Kate would not see what she had seen.

"Mother says it was too kind of me to write 'the silver gleams,'" she said.

Then their peace was shattered. John, James, Jean, and Ann came pounding up to join them.

"Kate's here," Jean accused Emily, "and you didn't tell us! We knew by her boots in the hall."

Emily had made the others sneak in and creep past the rooms where the four children were playing. Now she produced the cap, the canteen, a kaleidoscope, dress-up clothes. All were seized eagerly, but the children did not go away.

"You come and play with us!" Jean begged.

"I can't get Teddy's head back on this time," Ann said, really worried.

"We could *all* be explorers," James offered. "I'll let Kate carry the canteen. No, maybe I'd better. But I'll give you a drink, Kate, when you're dying on the desert."

Lindsay pushed the box of poems aside. She grinned good-naturedly at the four eager children.

"Come on, let's play with them," she said, sliding off the bed. "We can read this stuff any time."

Emily put her own poems back in the drawer. She should be thankful Lindsay did not mind.

She *was* thankful. But the poems . . . they meant more than that.

"Let's call ourselves The Quill Club," Kate said.

"Okay," Emily agreed.

Kate knew. Even though she loved the children as Emily herself did, even though she was already taking the part of an explorer, she did know the poems mattered.

"I'll be Sir Francis Drake," Emily cried. "But I'll need a sword, James."

He ran to get her a weapon.

15

Bloomfield's Books

October came. The leaves turned to gold. The kittens grew bigger hourly. After much discussion, they were named Velvet, Zebra, and Inky.

"Inky's my favorite." Kate cupped him in her palms and held him against her cheek. "I wish he were mine."

"Mother won't let us keep them." Emily bent to stroke Willie. "She says one cat is enough. Maybe, if you asked your mother, Kate—"

"No chance." Kate put the kitten back down. "Let's have a Club meeting."

The box Emily had so puzzled over no longer held their collected works. It was too small.

Each of them had her own notebook now. Emily kept the books in a trunk with a lock which her father had donated.

Lindsay had stopped writing poems. She wrote stories instead. Emily, listening, kept her face carefully blank, but at last Kate said bluntly, "Lin, those people aren't real. All that money and those crazy weddings with 'champagne flowing like water'! You don't know one single person like that."

Emily winced at Kate's frankness, but Lindsay remained unruffled.

"So what? I like them, real or not," she said. "I'm not trying to be the world's greatest writer like you and Emily, you know."

"But they're silly!"

"I like them silly," Lindsay said simply. "I like thinking about spending millions and millions of dollars."

Kate shook her head despairingly. Even Emily was embarrassed on Lindsay's behalf. But Lindsay, looking from one to the other, refused to give ground.

"I'll tell you both something," she said suddenly.

"You need me in this Club. You get so . . . so carried away sometimes. I keep you . . . I don't know . . . sensible or something."

Emily and Kate burst out laughing. Lindsay joined in. But she was right. Without her, they would sometimes have lost their balance.

"Well, let's hear some more about your crazy people," Kate grumbled, sitting back.

As Lindsay read on, Emily wondered what had made the others start a writing club in the first place. She took it for granted it had begun months before. Then, she was startled to hear Lindsay say, "That was last winter, before I knew Kate."

"I thought you'd both always lived here," she interrupted.

"We have," Lindsay said. "But Kate lived on the other side of town until this spring. I didn't even know she existed."

"Well, I didn't know you existed either." Kate laughed.

"That's what I'm saying. Then I finally got accelerated, and she finally moved into those apartments, and we were put in the same class in March."

"She still didn't know I existed," Kate told Emily.

"I did so," Lindsay defended herself. "I just thought. . . well, you seemed kind of . . . sort of . . ."

"Incorrigible?" suggested Emily with a sideways grin at Kate.

Lindsay went slightly pink.

"Not exactly—whatever that means," she said. "Just kind of different . . . like a tomboy or something.

"Incorrigible's the word all right," Kate nodded sagely. "But I won her over with my ladylike ways."

Emily looked at Kate, lolling against the foot of the bed. Her shirt had paint on it. Her hair needed cutting. It fell into her eyes and stuck up over her ears untidily. One of her shoes was untied. Both needed polishing. Her slacks were ripped on one knee. Emily could not suppress a snort of unladylike laughter.

"It was Laurel really," confessed Lindsay, with an abrupt burst of honesty. "She said, 'That Kate Bloomfield is the only interesting kid in your class,' so I thought I'd . . . well . . . see for myself, I guess."

"Thank you, Miss Lindsay Jane Ross." Kate stood up and bowed low.

"Quit that," Lindsay snapped, but, again, she was not really flustered.

All her life, she had been accepted, even pampered, by her entire family. She had never had to worry about what people thought of her. Now, without apologizing, she changed the subject.

"Have you been into Kate's bookstore yet?"

"No." Emily did not look at Kate. Bookstores drew her like a magnet, but, somehow, she had felt she should wait before going to this one.

"I have to go there when I leave here," Kate said. "I need some money for stuff for supper. You can come if you like."

"Okay," Emily said, not sure Kate wanted her.

She was afraid of this Kate. She was, once again, the Kate Emily had met that first night, the Kate who had cried out she wished Emily had never come to Riverside.

But they were friends now. Emily knew that.

"Let's go then." Kate slapped her notebook shut, shoved it onto Emily's desk, and was halfway to the door before Emily could gather her scattered thoughts.

"Thank you so much for urging me to stay, Emily, but I must be leaving," Lindsay said sweetly, grimacing at Kate's stiff back.

Kate did not bother to turn. She strode out into the hall, clattered down the stairs, snatched up her jacket, and marched out of the house. Emily, with a hurried wave at Lindsay, flew after her.

"Mother, I'm going out with Kate!" she called.

Hoping her mother had heard, she ran until she caught up with her friend.

Emily did not see Kate's parents at first. She stood stock-still, just inside the door of the store, and stared at the books. There were hundreds of them. The walls were lined with them. Revolving racks down the middle of the store held more. A couple of display tables were piled with recent fiction. Emily, who had loved books since she could remember, felt she had stepped into fairyland.

Straight down the aisle was a sign reading CHILDREN'S BOOKS. Unable to resist, she started toward them. Kate tugged her back.

"Mother," she said, "this is Emily Blair."

Mrs. Bloomfield looked like Kate. Emily saw that at first glance. The next moment, she wondered why she had thought so. Kate's mother had the same shape of face as her daughter. Her hair was the same rich brown. But while Kate stood at Emily's side in untidy clothes with her hair tumbling into her eyes, Mrs. Bloomfield was dressed in a lovely wool dress the color of a lime Popsicle. She had on dangling earrings, which were exactly the same shade of green, and her hair curled just so.

"I've heard so much about you, Emily," Mrs. Bloomfield began.

Emily felt her face grow hot. What was she supposed to say back?

"April," a voice called across the store, "do we have a copy of *The Return of the King?*"

"I sold the last one yesterday." Mrs. Bloomfield moved away from the two girls. "But we have *The Tolkien Reader* and the others. That one is on order."

"That's my father." Kate led the way back between the book racks.

Mrs. Bloomfield was still busy, and Emily once more veered towards the children's books.

"He's almost through." Kate grabbed her arm and held her back. "You don't have money for books anyway."

"I know I don't," Emily admitted, "but I still like looking."

There was *Charlotte's Web*. She already had that one. She had read it at least one hundred times! But were those the Narnia books? Could there be one she did not know about?

"I'll only be a minute," she said, and got away from Kate.

When Mr. Bloomfield was free, Emily had finished the first chapter of *Harriet the Spy*. She did not want to stop. Kate poked at her impatiently, but her father smiled in sympathy.

"It's a good book," he said. "I enjoyed it myself."

This time it was Kate's mother who interrupted.

"Mrs. Havergal says you promised to put away two copies of *The Scent of Water*, Slim, but I can't find them."

"They're in the back." Mr. Bloomfield went to get them.

"Come on, Emily," Kate said. "Mother gave me the money."

She left the bookstore quickly. Emily, however, paused long enough to look back through the glass door. Mrs. Bloomfield was watching her daughter go. The expression on her face startled Emily. She had seemed so busy. It had looked as though books were more important than talking to Kate and meeting her friend. Emily, still longing to go on with *Harriet the Spy*, could not help feeling that perhaps books did come first. At the same time, she remembered her mother meeting Kate. Mother had loved Kate from the beginning. Emily suspected that neither of the Bloomfields would be able to pick her, Emily, out of a group of girls her age.

She thought Kate's mother was going to call something after them. Her face was full of words she wanted to say. Emily did not know what the words were, but she recognized, without having to stop and think about it, that Mrs. Bloomfield cared about Kate as deeply as her own mother cared about her.

"I think your mother wants something," she said to Kate as the door latched behind them.

Kate glanced back through the pane. Mrs. Bloomfield had turned away.

"No, she doesn't," Kate said. "She and Slim won't be home for two hours. She already told me."

"You don't really call him Slim?" Emily half hoped she was wrong.

"Sometimes I do," bragged Kate. Then she grinned. "But not where he can hear me."

"I'll bet your mother *would* let you have Inky," Emily blurted as they came to the corner in front of her house and Kate turned to go home.

"No, she wouldn't," Kate said hopelessly.

"Listen, I didn't think Mother would let us keep Willie. But she did," Emily pressed on. "Yours probably doesn't know how badly you want him. Inky will be ready to go in a couple of weeks. Take him home and put him right into her hands. She won't be able to help loving him."

Kate thought about it, rubbing one toe along a crack in the sidewalk.

"I never tried that," she said slowly.

"Well, do." Emily sounded like her mother. "It will work. I'm positive."

"Okay. Maybe I will. Bye, Emily." Kate flashed her a luminous smile and ran off.

"Oh, Inky," Emily mourned, not wanting to give him up. Then she stood still and thought about Kate's mother again.

"I hope I'm right," she muttered, and crossed her fingers for luck.

16

A Home for Inky

Emily put away the last dish and went to get Inky ready. The other two kittens had already been given away, and Kate would arrive for him any minute now. But there was nothing she could do to make him more appealing. His sooty fur was softer than thistledown. His sea-green eyes watched the world with wonder. His minute black triangle of a nose quivered with curiosity. He wore his plump, plumy tail in a dozen different ways—wrapped primly around his paws, crooked in the air like a question mark, twitching with alarm, or poked up stiff and bristling as a bottlebrush when he made war.

Emily cradled him against her, her chin on top of his head.

"Oh, I don't want you to go," she whispered to him.

The kitten arched back and stretched a velvet paw to pat her cheek. She could not hear his purr—it was too soft—but she could feel him vibrating as though he had switched on a tiny motor inside.

"Here's Kate," Sophie announced.

Emily's hands moved automatically to thrust Inky back into the darkest corner of the box, out of sight. Then Kate came into the kitchen. Emily saw the worry in her eyes. Holding Inky out to her, she discovered, without surprise, that she cared more for Kate than she did for the kitten.

"It won't work," Kate said dismally, stroking him.

"It will so work," snapped Emily.

She went through the whole thing again. Kate listened and nodded, wanting to believe. She had imagined it happening the way Emily described, so often that now she had grown almost as sure as Emily.

Clutching Inky to her, Kate left, her head high—hoping, hoping.

Emily began her homework. She fought to keep her mind on her math problems. With one ear cocked for the ring of the telephone, she made little progress. Surely they must have said Yes by now!

It was the doorbell that rang.

Kate stood on the step, red-eyed and miserable. Inky, irresistible as ever, clung to her sweater and peered at Emily.

"But . . . but . . ." Emily stammered.

"She said 'No cat!'" Kate reported dully. "She said they shed hair and scratch the furniture. She said there'd be nobody home with him all day. She never even looked at him, not properly."

Emily was at a loss for words. If only she had not been so sure! Elizabeth Blair, coming to offer what comfort she could, heard Kate's explanation.

"Your mother is right, you know," Mrs. Blair told the girl quietly. "They do shed hair, and they do scratch furniture."

"Mother, you let us keep Wilhelmina Shakespeare!" Emily cried.

She, herself, had never hated anyone more than she hated Mrs. Bloomfield in that moment. She forgot about the look of love she had seen on Kate's mother's face in the store. She had always known that Kate's mother was mean!

"I wouldn't have but for Sophie," Mother reminded her. "She was so new to us then, and she loved Willie from the instant she saw her. But that's beside the point. We weren't living in a rented apartment, and someone is home here during the day. Emily, you aren't even trying to understand."

She looked from her daughter's stubborn face

to Kate's unhappy one and gave up attempting to make them see Mrs. Bloomfield's point of view. Something else was needed now.

"Kate Bloomfield," she said, her voice deliberately light, almost teasing, "how would you like to have this foolish Inky for your own personal cat—only he can board here with us instead of at your place. Goodness knows, we've cat hair all over anyway, and the furniture is past help."

Kate lifted her head. She stared at Emily's mother, not really understanding.

"You mean, we keep him—but he's really Kate's?" Emily got it clear.

"Isn't that what I said?" Mrs. Blair smiled, but she was watching Kate.

"Really mine," the girl said slowly.

"Well, yours and Wilhelmina Shakespeare's," Mother promised.

"Oh, Inky," Kate breathed. Her eyes filled with tears.

"Don't cry, dopey," Emily said.

"I'm not." Kate hid her face in Inky's fur.

Two days later, she arrived at school in a new green jumper with pockets. Although she was supposed to hate girls' things, she revolved slowly in front of Lindsay and Emily, letting them get the full beauty of it. She had a new blouse to go with it, and matching stockings.

"Was it your birthday?" Emily knew Kate had had new clothes to start school.

"No." Kate frowned, pleating the soft material between her fingers. When she looked up, her eyes were troubled.

"I think Mother felt sorry about Inky," she said.

Emily struggled with this fact. Mrs. Bloomfield had seemed an ogre. Was she only an ordinary mother after all?

"Dad too," Kate mumbled. "He brought me home *Up a Road Slowly* last night."

"He . . . what?" Emily said.

"It's a book," Lindsay told her smugly. "I saw it in the library. I wish my mother and father felt sorry like that," she finished, turning back to Kate.

"I'd rather have had Inky," Kate said, stubborn in her disappointment.

Yet she walked proudly in her pretty new clothes, and Emily knew that she was pleased with her parents' concern.

The bright leaves blew down from the trees. November, cold and grey, walked the streets of Riverside. December came and the first snowfall. Often Aunt Deborah wrote to the four children and they wrote back, telling Emily what to say. Ann had trouble remembering her mother clearly, but the others worked hard at reminding her. They were worried lest their mother would come back to discover that Ann did not know who she was. Emily, listening to them, helping with the letters, tried to wish Aunt Deborah would hurry and get well. But, however hard she tried, most of her could not escape knowing that everything must change when Aunt Deborah came home. Emily did not want things to change.

At least nobody knows, she told herself.

But Mrs. Blair saw more than Emily imagined.

Christmas was coming, coming, coming! Plans were being made left and right. Laurel Ross had Christmas Day off and was coming home. The Bloomfields had finally decided they would go to Calgary to see their grandson, and Kate was not sure whether to be elated or scared at the thought of flying in a plane. Elizabeth Blair, to her family's amazement, had actually persuaded old Mrs. Thurstone to spend Christmas Day with them.

"What did she really say?" Dad prodded.

"It's not the words that matter," Mother evaded. "It's the feeling behind them."

"Elizabeth, tell me her exact words."

Mother laughed and gave in.

"She said, 'Spend Christmas in that madhouse? I never heard such a ridiculous idea in all my born days. But I'll come. Somebody with sense should be there when one of those children knocks over the Christmas tree or some such foolishness.'"

"Very thoughtful of her," Dad commented, putting his arm around his wife and holding her against him.

"Let me go," Mother said.

"Fiddlesticks," Dad answered, grinning at the children.

When The Quill Club met the next afternoon, Emily was ablaze with a new idea.

"Listen," she burst out before the other two were settled, "why don't we write a Christmas play? The kids could put it on. Jean could be Mary, and John could be Joseph—"

"And James could be the Baby Jesus, I suppose." Lindsay giggled.

Kate did not say anything.

Emily, who had expected Kate to understand and welcome her idea at once, was disappointed. She waited an instant longer. Still Kate made no response.

She, Emily, would have to make it clearer, that was all. How could even Kate grasp something flung at her so suddenly? But how could she explain? They would have to have been there from the beginning.

It had started the night before when she was lying in bed, looking up through her window at her own star. It had shone down so brightly at her out of the looming darkness.

"Maybe the Christmas Star looked like that," she had murmured dreamily. "Small, but bright and special."

The thought loosed her imagination. Without actually stirring from under her warm covers, she found herself far away and long ago. She stood at the bottom of a hill. At the top of it, in the night sky, her star was waiting—only somehow she knew it was not just hers any longer. She started up the narrow, lonely road towards it, following its beauty, and as she went the road around her filled with all the people she knew. They did not speak. They were just there—first her mother, then Jean and Ann hand in hand, then Kate carrying a lamb as tenderly as she would Inky. They were all wearing the kind of clothes she had seen in Bible pictures—long cloaks and hoods, and sandals on their feet. She was not surprised even when she looked down and found she, too, was dressed in a rough brown skirt that reached to her toes.

"We must be going to find the real Christmas," she thought—and she smiled at Kate.

Then it was over. She was back in the bed she had never really left. Still, her moment of inner vision stayed clear and bright in her mind. First, she tried to turn it into a poem. Then suddenly she decided it must be a play. Instead of the starry uphill road, she had begun to see their own attic, transformed with homemade scenery into Bethlehem. Snatches of singing words came to her. It had all been vague, but so beautiful.

"No, but, really, I'm serious," she said at last, answering Lindsay but speaking directly to Kate. "We could be in it too. Maybe it could be about a boy shepherd or . . . well, we'd have to work out things like that. All three of us could write the words."

Surely Kate would understand. Lindsay would do whatever Kate did, Emily knew. But Kate was still silent.

"Maybe we could call it 'Under a Special Star' or something," Emily forged ahead, feeling more and more uncomfortable for no reason she could understand. "Kate . . . ?" she appealed at last.

"It's pretty late to write a play like that," said Kate. Nothing in Kate's muffled words responded to Emily's eagerness. "I don't think I'd be much good at writing a play anyway . . ." She trailed off.

Something was wrong. Kate had stopped speaking, but her last sentence hung in the air, unfinished. She had something more to say. But she doesn't want to say it, Emily guessed.

Don't be crazy, she told herself, fighting off sudden panic. What *could* be wrong?

But, darting a glance at Lindsay, she saw her own uncertainty mirrored on the other girl's face.

Kate raised her head and confronted the pair of them. Her chin jutted out at a defiant angle, but her eyes looked beyond them at Emily's bedroom wall.

"I guess I shouldn't help write a Christmas play anyway," she said at last, her stiff voice sounding like that of a stranger. "I'm part Jewish, you know."

17

Trouble Ahead

"Part Jewish," Emily repeated after what seemed forever. "What do you mean, 'part Jewish'?"

Lindsay looked as startled as she did, Emily saw. Lindsay had not known this either.

"It's hard to explain," Kate said. "I was going to tell you before . . . but . . . I didn't know what you'd think."

"What we'd think," Emily echoed.

She felt stupid, as though she should be thinking a certain kind of thought, but she did not know what thought to think. She did not know the right words to say either.

Emily had never, knowingly, met anyone who

was Jewish. Jews, to her, meant people out of
the Bible—and Kate, in her old plaid skirt and
scuffed shoes, with her too-long brown hair and
familiar face, did not look like anybody Emily
had ever imagined belonging in a Bible story.

Kate sighed, sat straighter, and began to try
to explain.

Her father was Jewish.

"At least, he used to be," Kate said uneasily. "I
guess he still is. He says he is."

His parents had been strict people, Orthodox
in their religion, upright and unyielding, hard
for a boy to understand. He had been brought
up to attend the synagogue regularly. He had
been sent to Hebrew class after school.

"And he was Bar Mitzvah when he was thir-
teen," Kate told them.

"What?" Lindsay said.

Emily nudged her to be quiet. It was hard
enough for Kate, she could see. Her face was
strained, and her voice was louder than usual.

Lindsay scowled at Emily but subsided for
the moment. Kate went doggedly on.

"They used to fight a lot, I think. Anyway, he
left home when he was nineteen and he got a
job. He had lots of different kinds of jobs. He
met my mother when he was twenty."

"What's your mother?" Lindsay asked, leaning
forward a little, not looking at Emily.

"Mother? She's nothing. I mean, she doesn't
go to a church," Kate floundered. "By the time

they got married, my father had stopped going to the synagogue too. We don't go to a church or a synagogue, either one. My mother says if Sunday's a 'day of rest,' she's going to rest on it."

There was a spark of pride in Kate's voice as she quoted her mother. Emily could see why. To her, too, they sounded like daring words.

"I think her parents were Anglicans, or something," Kate added vaguely. "But there wasn't a church near them . . . I don't know. They got married at the City Hall."

"But where were you baptized?" Lindsay had more questions ready. "And where did your sister get married?"

"I wasn't baptized," Kate replied stonily, "and Marilyn was married in a church. Her husband's a Presbyterian."

"I don't think you're really Jewish at all." Lindsay reached out and patted Kate's limp hand as though she, Lindsay, were years older than the other girl. "It's not as though you were a Catholic or something like that. You're just nothing. When you grow up, you can be whatever you want."

Emily had sat listening silently, trying hard to understand. Now a sentence of Lindsay's caught her attention.

"The Sutherland kids are Catholics," she said, giving Lindsay a level look.

Lindsay, her eyes wide, turned from Kate.

"They ARE?" she gasped. "But they just seem like ordinary children. I mean . . . "

"What church do you go to, Lindsay?" pursued Emily.

"The United."

"Well, we're Presbyterians," Emily countered. "And my mother stays home from church lots of Sundays and rests too."

The three girls looked at one another. Finally, Emily found words for their confusion. With a sense of discovery, she said simply, "It doesn't make one bit of difference. It didn't before we knew—so why should it now? We're the same people we were ten minutes ago."

"But if your cousins are Roman Catholics!" protested Lindsay, still finding that hard to believe.

"And I'm nothing," Kate added, with a glimmer of a grin.

"It does not make one particle of difference," Emily insisted. "We could even write my play about the first Christmas. You know, Lin, there weren't any United Church people there. Just Jews!"

"Emily!" Lindsay protested.

But Emily was beginning to enjoy herself.

"I'll bet plenty of them didn't believe that baby was anything special either," she said.

She turned directly to Kate then. "You could always play King Herod. That would make you Jewish clear through instead of just half and half. He was wicked, of course. I think you'd be perfect for the part."

She herself did not understand what she was doing. She heard, with a mixture of horror and awe, words spilling out of her mouth. Reckless words, words with power to hurt. Yet, somehow, she had to make Kate stop looking as though she felt like an outsider.

"You can play King Herod your own self," Kate said. Her grin was crooked but real. The tight, shuttered look left her eyes. Within Emily, a matching knot of tension eased. What the danger had been she was not sure, but they had passed it together.

Now Lindsay was the one who felt shut out. The discovery that the Sutherlands were Catholics had jolted her. All Emily's nonsense about King Herod did not change this. Lindsay's grandfather went on and on about Catholics when he came to visit the Rosses. "Papists" he called them. From him, Lindsay had put together a picture of a Catholic. Hadn't he said they "worshipped idols"? Something like that, she was certain.

"Don't they bow down to saints and think Mary is better than God? Catholics I mean," she said.

"Can you imagine James bowing down to a saint?" Emily laughed at her. "They *do* think Mary's special—but not better than God, Lin. Who told you that? She must have been special. After all, she brought Jesus up, didn't she?"

Lindsay looked thoughtful. Kate studied

Emily with admiration. Neither of them realized that she was so ready with her answers only because she and her mother had talked some of these things over when the Sutherland children came to live with the Blairs. During the months since, Emily had seen for herself that she and her four small cousins were more alike than different.

"Okay," Lindsay said slowly at last. "But I don't know about this play of yours. Like Kate says, we wouldn't have much time to write it— and the kids would have to learn their lines."

An inner voice told Emily that Lindsay was right and, more important, that Kate was unhappy with the whole idea.

But Emily would not listen, not yet. The play was still there in her mind's eye. The details were hazy but the feeling was so clear, so perfect. She ached to see it become a reality. She could deal with the problems Lindsay raised. She ignored Kate's uneasiness. They understood each other now. There was nothing to worry about. The danger was over.

"We can make it a pageant," she said hurriedly, getting paper and pencils for all three of them. "Then there won't be lines to learn. One of us can be the narrator. How'll we start?"

Watching Emily's rush to begin, Kate guessed what the play meant to her. She too had had ideas like that. Because she did understand and because Emily had known so clearly that Kate was still Kate, whether she was "part Jewish" or not, Kate did not back out. And when Kate and Emily took up a project, Lindsay automatically took it up too. They were The Quill Club, after all.

It went badly. They had never tried to write anything together before. They worked so differently. It was impossible for them to agree even on the opening sentence.

Kate knew the Christmas story, but she could not help thinking of bitter things she had heard her father say about the commercialism of Christmas. "More grabbing than giving," he said. When carols came over the radio or there were special programs on television, he switched them off abruptly and buried himself behind a book. For Emily's sake, Kate had determined to try. But she was not happy about it.

"This is terrible!" Emily said at last in disgust.

Underneath her disgust was despair. The star she had seen, the travelers down the road, the inn in Bethlehem—none of them was here in these bungled phrases.

"Girls, time to go home," Mrs. Blair called from the bottom of the stairs.

Kate and Lindsay jumped up, glad to escape. But Emily was not quite ready to give up yet.

"I have to go to church in the morning," she began.

"Yeah, me too," Lindsay agreed.

Kate's silence was louder than any speech.

"What I meant was, we can go on with it

tomorrow afternoon," Emily stammered, her cheeks hot.

"I guess so," said Lindsay without eagerness.

Kate just nodded. She and Lindsay left.

Emily stood alone in the hall after the door had closed behind them.

She doesn't mind, she told herself. Why should she?

It was no use. Every atom of her knew that Kate did mind. She did not know yet how she would tell the others, but she knew, that instant, that they could not go on with the play.

It wouldn't have worked anyway, she thought, remembering their false starts. I don't mind us quitting. I'm even glad!

She *was* glad. Relieved anyway. But, whatever she told herself, Emily was like Kate. She still minded.

18

No Easy Answers

The next morning, Kate sat at home, wishing she had Inky to play with, thinking of the other two girls in their churches. Her mother was still asleep, but her father sat across the room from her.

"Reading as usual," Kate muttered to herself.

If only she could talk to him! Really talk. Tell him what had happened yesterday at the Blairs and ask him . . .

Suddenly, it was as though Emily were there beside her—Emily who had been so sure she would be allowed to have a kitten, Emily who dared to take chances.

"Dad," Kate said. Her voice came out huskily,

and she gave a nervous cough. Maybe he had not even heard her.

"Yes, Katharine," he answered.

He did not put down his book. Kate's courage ebbed away. Then—as she was to tell Emily days later—she made herself think of her again, deliberately.

"Go ON!" Emily's voice urged, although Emily was, in fact, standing in the Presbyterian church singing "Faith of Our Fathers." "Talk to him."

"What are you reading?" Kate asked.

Now why had she asked him *that?* He, too, was puzzled. He actually looked up at her over the book.

"Darkness at Noon," he answered. His answer sounded more like a question, but Kate was not ready for it.

"Would I like it?" she asked desperately, having no idea how to find out what she really wanted to know.

"No, not yet," he said, but slowly, as though he were giving it careful consideration. "It isn't a book you'd like—though it's a book you'll probably want to read someday."

"Is the person who wrote it Jewish?" Kate burst out.

Jonathan Bloomfield half-closed the book, although his finger still kept the place.

"Why do you ask, Katharine?" he questioned quietly.

"What I really want to know is . . ." Kate floundered, dropping all pretense of interest in the book, " . . . well . . . am I Jewish?"

"Not so's you'd notice." Her father smiled, looking at her. Her troubled face sobered him in the next instant, and he frowned at his own words. Then he put the book down on the arm of his chair, actually losing his place.

"That's not answering your question at all," he admitted. "I just meant that you look like your mother. But many Jewish people, devout, Orthodox Jews, don't look like me. I, Katharine, 'look Jewish.' "

Kate gazed at him—his black hair thinning on top, his dark humorous eyes, his beak of a nose, and his rueful smile. He weighed more than he should. Was this how Jewish people looked?

"It doesn't prove a thing," he told her, without her having to ask. "Lots of devout, orthodox Christians look like me. But when a gentile thinks of a Jew—"

"Is Emily a gentile?" Kate interrupted, in spite of herself.

She was sitting facing him now, her chin in her hands, her face excited. Why hadn't she talked to him long ago?

"Emily. . ." Mr. Bloomfield looked confused. Then he remembered. Emily would have been surprised to know how clearly he recalled her face, enchanted and still, bent above *Harriet the Spy*. "Is she the child who started *Harriet*?"

"Started Harriet?" It was Kate who had forgotten.

"Never mind. I do remember her. Get the dictionary, Kate."

Kate might have known. They were forever consulting a dictionary in her house. She fetched one, found "gentile" and read aloud, "'Person not of the Jewish race, heathen, pagan.'"

Mr. Bloomfield sighed and rubbed one ear.

"Look up 'Jew,'" he said, not much hope in his voice.

"'Person of Hebrew race,'" Kate read.

"Well, they let me down," her father commented wryly.

"Dad, we learned in school about races, and there are only three—"

"I'm sure you did, and they're absolutely right." He did not wait for her to finish. He seemed to have only half his thoughts on what he himself was saying. Suddenly he leaned forward and looked at her intently, as though he had something of special importance to tell her. Kate sat and listened with her whole being.

"Kate, I can't answer the question you're really asking." He weighed each word. "Being Jewish is so many things to so many people. For some, it is an entire way of life—an ethic, a form of worship, different food, or food prepared in a special way, a distinctive language sometimes. It is a world where only other Jews sharing that way of life belong. I was brought up in that world—and I came away and left it." He paused.

He looks sad, Kate thought. She did not move.

"When I broke with my family, I parted with much that was good and meaningful. I am still often lonely for the life I knew as a boy. I didn't have to ask the question you ask now. My identity was made plain to me at every turn."

"But—" Kate started. She was silent again, seeing he had halted simply to clarify what he sought to tell her.

"I'm lonely, but I wouldn't go back," he said. "Your mother and I care deeply for each other. We have made our own life—and, for us, it is good. We can't tell you the answers to the big questions, Katharine. 'Who are we?' 'Why are we here?' 'Is there a God?' 'Is He concerned about us?' But that is the exciting thing about being a human being. Or one of the exciting things. The questions are always there."

"But the answers!" Kate protested, wanting something to hold on to.

"The answers—ah!" Mr. Bloomfield sat back. His eyes twinkled at her, but he was still serious, Kate knew. "Those are what life is all about. You find part of an answer—and it leads to another question. Never does the wonder, the asking, end."

"I still don't know if I'm Jewish or not," Kate broke in.

Her voice sounded hard and stubborn, but her father had reached for his book. She wanted help. If only he would make everything plain, simple.

"That is something you'll spend your whole life finding out, Katharine," he told her gently. "Orthodox Jews will tell you No. Gentiles—and Emily *is* a gentile, to answer your earlier query—will tell you Yes. You can be proud to be Jewish. I am. But you are your mother's daughter too."

He fanned through the book, found the page where he had ceased reading, scanned a sentence. Kate, confused, a little angry, and deeply pleased with what had happened between them, rose to go. He lowered the book once more then, and looked up at her, this child of his with her mixed heritage.

"You're lucky, Kate," he said. "You already know you don't know who you are. Many people don't discover that till they're middle-aged."

"Emily—a heathen! I must tell her," Kate grinned, closing the dictionary.

"Emily is Emily," Mr. Bloomfield said sternly. "You keep that fact firmly in mind. Prejudice works in all of us, and it's a subtle, cruel thing. Stupid too. I wouldn't want you stupid—especially if you're Jewish!"

"Don't worry," Kate shot back. She felt lighter than air as she left him there, reading. She had so many other things she wanted to talk to him about. There would be time. Now she had started, there would be time.

Not that he's much help, she said to herself.

She walked proudly, though, knowing he was hers.

19

What's Wrong, Emily?

The Blairs were at lunch when Mrs. Ross phoned. Mother went. The family paid no attention till they heard Elizabeth Blair exclaim, "It can't be true!"

They all eavesdropped after that, but they only heard:

"How is she?"

"Oh, dear . . . what did he say?"

"Two to three weeks!"

"I don't know whom I'm sorriest for. Of course, I'll tell Kate too. Emily definitely hasn't had them but maybe . . ."

"Let me know if there's anything I can do."

When she returned to the dining room, they were waiting.

"Lindsay Ross has chicken pox," Mother announced.

"You sound like Chicken Little," Dad told her. "The sky is falling! The sky is falling!"

"I *feel* like Chicken Little," Mother said in a voice of deep gloom. "You *do* realize that Emily's never had them, and in two to three weeks we'll be right smack in the middle of Christmas!"

Uncle Roger was there for the weekend. He gave his sister a rueful look.

"I hate to mention this," he began, "but—"

"We've never had them too!" James finished for him.

"Roger, you're joking?"

"I wish I were."

Emily finished her last bite of pie. She tried to look dismayed, but she could not quite manage it. Here was a perfect reason for giving up the play. She thought of Kate. Since the day before, she could not seem to stop thinking of Kate.

"Emily, are you feeling all right?" her mother asked as they did the dishes together.

"Sure. Why wouldn't I be?"

Mrs. Blair looked at her and did not pursue it. But when the dishes were put away, Emily lingered in the kitchen. She and her mother were alone for a change. Uncle Roger and Sophie had taken the Sutherland children and their sleds to the park. Dad was reading in the living room.

Elizabeth Blair hung up the dishcloth and started to leave. Then she glanced once more at her daughter's face and changed her mind. She did have two white shirts she had put off ironing. Now was as good a time as any.

"Remember the Sabbath Day," she muttered to herself and reached for the first one.

"Mother," Emily burst out at last, "did you know Kate's Jewish—part Jewish anyway," she amended.

"No." Mrs. Blair began to iron as though her daughter had said nothing out of the ordinary, but Emily, watching, saw her expression change.

As if I'd asked where babies come from, Emily thought with interest.

"How did she come to tell you this? It *was* Kate who told you, I take it?"

"Yes." Emily hesitated, not wanting to speak of the play. Finally, skipping that part of it altogether, she told her mother what Kate had told them about her parents. Mrs. Blair busied herself with the shirt and waited. When Emily stood silently, fiddling with the bottom button on her sweater, her mother took a deep breath and pried.

"What's wrong, Emily?"

"Kate said she didn't tell us before because she didn't know what we'd think." She jerked at the button until it was in danger of coming loose. Then she left it alone, straddled a chair, and looked up at Mother. "What's *wrong* with being Jewish anyway?"

"There's nothing wrong with being Jewish," Elizabeth Blair stated.

She was angry, Emily could tell. She also knew that the anger was not directed at herself or at Kate. Silence grew between them. Emily did not know what to ask next. Her mother had sounded so sure there was nothing wrong, but Kate . . . She raised grave eyes and met her mother's gaze.

"Oh, I'm dodging, Emily," Mrs. Blair said, thumping her iron down and turning the shirt around. "I know it. I'm telling you the truth, but I'm avoiding your question. You want to know why Kate found it hard to tell you she was Jewish. Well, many people *do* think there's 'something wrong' with being a Jew. Many people have deep and terrible prejudices against Jews. Many people feel there's something wrong with being Catholic or Protestant or black or native or American too. The reasons for prejudice go away back in history. Superstition, ignorance, envy—"

"But, Mother, what does all that have to do with Kate?"

Elizabeth Blair stopped in mid-sentence and looked startled. Then she said simply, "Not a thing—except she'll have to live in the world, and she'll sometimes meet ugliness in people who won't take the trouble to know her but will avoid or dislike her simply because she's Jewish."

Emily was aghast.

"That's not fair," she cried.

"No," her mother agreed. She took the other shirt out of the basket and spread it out.

"Emily, did you realize that Ruth was Jewish?" she asked then.

It took Emily a moment to remember who Ruth was.

"Jewish . . . Ruth?" she said. "But she's not a bit like Kate."

"Thank goodness. Ruth was such a whiner."

"Mo-ther!" Emily was shocked. She had not liked Ruth much either, but if Ruth was Jewish . . .

Mrs. Blair laughed at her.

"Emily, Emily, what do you think I'm trying to tell you," she said. "Ruth didn't whine because she was Jewish but because she was Ruth and she'd learned to get her own way by whining. Think this over for a moment. Suppose you *had* known Ruth was Jewish, and she was the first Jewish child you'd met. Would you have said to yourself 'So *this* is what Jewish people are like'?"

Emily tried hard to believe she would not, but she could see that it could happen.

"I used to hope you wouldn't find out," her mother told her. "Remember Sharon?"

"Yes," Emily said, round-eyed, thinking of fat, bossy Sharon who picked her nose and was a tattletale. "Was she Jewish too?"

Mother grinned.

"No. She was a Presbyterian—just like you. A Jewish child, getting to know Sharon, might also have come to some odd conclusions."

Emily nodded. She felt a bit stunned.

"The world's a mixed-up place, Emily, and prejudices are a part of it—and a part of you and me, whether we like it or not. Some people are prejudiced against us, too, of course."

"Against us?" Emily could not believe it. She had done nothing . . .

"We're white," her mother said, "and we're Christians. We belong to the middle class—although if your father buys any more houses, we won't for long. We're all sorts of things lots of people don't like."

"But what do we *do* about it?" Emily wanted to know.

"We go on being ourselves, I guess. We try to get to know all kinds of people. We fight prejudice when we meet it—in others or in ourselves. We concentrate on the Kates and forget the Ruths. No, that's not right either. We—"

"Okay, okay!" Emily jumped up, seeing what was coming. "Don't tell me nobody understands Ruth and all that stuff. I don't mind her. But this whole thing is just plain dumb, if you ask me."

"Granted," Elizabeth Blair said promptly.

"What?"

"Granted. You're right. That's obvious."

Emily turned back.

"If it's so obvious—" she started.

"It's not obvious to everyone. It's only obvious to you because you've looked through Kate's window," her mother answered.

Emily stared at her. Her own small window with its shining star came into her mind, but that had nothing to do with Kate.

"Haven't you ever heard that expression? No? Perhaps not. My grandmother used to use it. Whenever one of us would say 'I just cannot understand what makes her act like that!' she'd say 'Well, look through her window for a while—and it'll come clear.' It's like 'walk in her shoes' or 'try seeing it through her eyes.' Your life is one window on the world, and Kate's is another. Because you're friends—real friends— you've looked through her window, and enlarged your own world. Do you understand me, Emily?"

"Of course I do," her daughter said impatiently.

"Good—because there's the doorbell. Break it gently to Kate about the chicken pox. Let's pray that she, at least, had sense enough to get them over with years ago."

But Kate had not had them either.

20

Mother to the Rescue

"How'll I tell my mother?" she wailed when Emily greeted her with the news.

Emily, seeing how real Kate's dismay was, led the way back out to the kitchen. Her own mother had vanished with the shirts she had ironed, but she would be back. Emily had learned, years ago, that if she wanted her mother, the kitchen was the best place to lie in wait. She gave Kate a chair and tried to cheer her up.

"Just tell her," she advised, not yet understanding Kate's predicament. "She'll survive. Mine did."

"Yours hasn't made reservations on a flight to Calgary on the twentieth," Kate said.

Emily began to see.

"If I tell her now—just when everything is extra complicated at the store because they're leaving—she'll get in a snit. And then maybe I won't even get them," Kate went on, thinking out loud. "But suppose I don't tell her—and the day before we're to leave I wake up covered with them. She'll DIE!"

"Maybe you could go anyway," Emily offered for want of something better to say.

Kate did not bother to answer. They both knew you did not fly Air Canada with chicken pox. Besides, in Calgary there was Kate's sister's baby.

Mother returned and looked at Kate's stricken face.

"Don't tell me. Let me guess," she began.

"Stop fooling, Mother. This is serious." Emily interrupted and explained.

"Maybe I'm immune or something." Kate tried to sound hopeful.

"We were with Lindsay, though, all yesterday afternoon," remembered Emily.

Kate looked dejected again. "I already thought of that," she admitted.

Mother pulled out a chair and sat down with them.

"Kate, what are you stewing about?" she said gaily, ruefully. "If you get them, you simply come over and join the rest of us. My nieces and nephews would never let me miss an opportunity like this. They have given me every kind of experience they can think of. Now it's to be an epidemic. Well, I'm a stronger, wiser woman than I once was, and I can handle anything—flood, fire, famine, drought. You'd hardly be noticed."

Kate looked at Emily's mother. She thought she had heard an invitation to come to the Blairs, but, what with "flood, fire, famine and drought," she was not sure.

"Perfect!" Emily cried, understanding at once. "Oh, Mother, that would be great. I hope Kate does get chicken pox!"

"Emily Blair!" her mother said, but she was not really shocked.

Kate beamed shyly at them both. She had no words to say what was in her heart. Yet a second later her face clouded.

"It'll be Christmas though," she said. "If I came, we . . . I . . ."

"Don't you have Christmas?" Emily was swept with amazement and pity.

Kate had been staring down at her hands clenched in her lap. Hearing all Emily did not say, she lifted her head. Deliberately, she undid her fists and clasped her hands loosely on top of the table.

"My father doesn't like it, but we do have a tree and give gifts. We don't make a big thing out of it. We don't sing carols or anything like that."

She spoke evenly. A spark in her eyes warned them she wanted no sympathy.

Elizabeth Blair did not offer any. She simply put one arm lightly around the straight young shoulders.

"Kate," she said, "Christmas, to us, means loving each other. More than anything else, that's what it means. Oh, we'll sing carols, and we'll read the Christmas story—and sometimes, if you're with us, you may feel different. But so will Sophie. Mrs. Thurstone will be lonely too. And the children and Roger—last year Deborah was with them. If we have chicken pox on top of everything else . . . But I'm like Emily. I almost hope you *do* get chicken pox. You'll add so much to our Christmas."

Kate rubbed the back of her hand across her eyes.

"Okay then," she said. "I . . . I'll let you know."

The three of them laughed unsteadily, and it was settled.

A week went by. No chicken pox.

"We won't get them." Emily was more disappointed than relieved.

"Don't discount your chicken pox before they're hatched," quipped her father.

Another day passed safely. Another. Christmas was only a week away. The Bloomfields were leaving the day after tomorrow.

"Emily, telephone," Mother called.

"Hello."

"I have them," Kate said. "They're like pimples. My mother is frantic. What'll I do?"

"I'll send my mother over right away," Emily promised.

Mother put her coat on immediately.

"If I'd met the woman just once, it would help," she muttered, bending over to pull on her boots.

"I've met her," Emily said.

"You have! I didn't know that. What's she like?" Mother straightened up and waited, studying her daughter's face.

"I don't know. She's okay I guess," Emily said helplessly.

"Well, where did you meet her?" Mrs. Blair persisted, trying to get some clue to the kind of person she was about to face.

"At the store. Mr. Bloomfield was there too. Her name is April," Emily offered, brightening.

"That should be a great help," her mother said dryly. "Did you like her?"

"Yes," Emily said. "At least, I sort of did."

Mrs. Blair looked exasperated.

"I can't imagine what I'd do without you, Emily," she said. "I just cannot imagine. I must leave, or Kate will think we're deserting her. Keep things going till I get back."

Emily paced up and down. Time crawled. Mother had been gone almost an hour. What on earth was going on over there?

Ann, sobbing noisily, came to find her.

"Jean won't play with me!"

"Don't cry." Emily soothed her automatically. "Would you like a drink of milk?"

"But, Emily, Jean—" Ann began again.

Emily hoisted her into her arms and carried

her to the kitchen. Ann, seeing her cousin was paying no attention, hushed. They were still there when the front door slammed. Emily left the little girl without a backward glance and ran to meet her mother.

"What did she say?" she asked breathlessly.

Then she gasped with delight and laughter mingled.

Kate, suitcase in hand and chicken pox all over her face, stood in the hall. Emily flung her arms around her. Ten minutes later, the two of them were in Emily's room, unpacking Kate's belongings. Mrs. Blair had agreed, after a short argument, that Emily could sleep on the floor on an air mattress and Kate could have the bed. That way, they could be together.

"But what *did* your mother say?" Emily asked again as Kate began to put one of her dresses on a hanger.

"She said, 'Thank God!'" Kate told her. Her hands stilled as she remembered. "Just like that. 'Thank God!' As though your mother were an answer to a prayer or something."

"Where were you?" Emily settled down to hear the whole story. Kate dropped the dress and launched into it.

"I was in the bathroom when she first came in. I could hear Mother say that right through the door. By the time I got out there, she was crying!"

"Crying!"

"Really. And she told your mother all kinds of things I never knew. I didn't get it straight, but there's something wrong with Marilyn's baby. Is there such a thing as a hole in the heart?"

Emily shrugged. Kate went sweeping on.

"Well, it's something like that. Marilyn's made herself sick, worrying about him, and David—he's her husband—wrote and asked Mother to please come. Dad kept trying to help Mother tell it, and your mother sat down and held my mother's hand. Next thing I knew, YOUR mother was crying."

"My mother!"

"Not like mine—but she had tears on her face. I saw them. It was awful, in a way, but exciting too. Like a movie. Then they talked about all my mother has to do before they go and who would look after me because she and Dad have to be at the store. She was going on about us not having relatives. And your mother said, 'Why not let me take her home with me tonight?' She said she had help." Kate giggled shakily. "She made Sophie sound like an army of people."

"Sophie's better than an army when you need help," Emily said.

"Anyway, my mother cried harder than ever and said she wanted to look after me herself!" Kate's eyes shone as she repeated these words. "But your mother talked some more and so did my father—and then the two of them, our mothers I mean, packed up my stuff—and here I am. And your mother really liked my mother," Kate said wonderingly.

Emily smiled at the other girl. She could see the whole thing happening as Kate described it. Mrs. Bloomfield sounded tired and worried and real. Not an ogre after all!

"Of course she does," said Emily. "Why wouldn't she?"

Kate looked at her strangely. "What's that on your forehead?"

Emily put her hand up. There was nothing there.

"I don't know what you mean," she said, staring back at Kate.

Her mother blew into the room like a whisk of wind.

"Emily Ann Blair, this child is sick and ought to be in her bed," she scolded. "And you keep her up talking. Kate, get into your pajamas this instant."

"Mrs. Blair," Kate said, "look at Emily's forehead."

Mother glanced at Emily. She looked again, harder.

"All right, Miss Bloomfield, I see them," she said. "Emily, you get ready for bed too, right now."

"But why . . . ?" Emily started.

"You have chicken pox, lame-brain!" Kate answered, choking with laughter.

Emily sprang up and ran to the mirror. Kate

was right. They did look like pimples. There were three of them on her forehead and another on her ear.

"I'm sure Ann has a fever." Mrs. Blair talked on as though Emily were the least of her worries. "She'll have them in the morning. Jean and James seem all right, but I can't find John anywhere."

"Maybe he's in his room," Emily suggested, not really listening.

Her mother went to check. Emily turned to Kate.

"Did Mother call your mother April?" she could not resist asking.

"Just at the end," Kate nodded.

"Did she call your father Slim?"

"No," Kate grinned. "My mother's the only person who calls him that. She says he used to be slim when she first knew him."

"Land of liberty, a child with sense!" Elizabeth Blair cried from across the hall.

The girls hurried to investigate.

John Sutherland was in bed, in his pajamas, sound asleep, his flushed cheeks dotted with chicken pox.

21

The Days Before Christmas

By the time Mr. and Mrs. Bloomfield left for Calgary, all six children at the Blairs' had chicken pox. Mrs. Bloomfield came over the night before, her arms laden with gifts.

"Oh, I shouldn't go!" she cried, looking around at the ring of spotty faces.

"Don't be silly," Mother told her. "Sophie's here—and those girls aren't too sick to help."

"Won't Sophie be going somewhere else for Christmas though?" Mrs. Bloomfield asked.

"No. Her brother and his wife went on a trip to New York," Mother explained. She did not say what she thought of Sophie's brother for not inviting Sophie to go along, but it was plain in her face.

"Be thankful," the other woman advised her. "Just be thankful."

"I am," Mother said, her heart in the words.

With Christmas so close, the children recovered with the speed of light. This just was no time to be sick. They had to trim the tree and wrap presents. Every one of them had something hidden away, some last minute gift to get ready.

Emily had her own secret project. She was putting together a book of her own poems for Kate. Most of them were poems Kate had already read, but Emily was working, inside her head, on two special new ones about Kate herself.

She thought it would be awkward finding time to work on them without Kate near, but, to her surprise, Kate, too, seemed to want time alone.

Finally, both poems were done. Emily, by herself in her bedroom, pored over them. They seemed right—or as right as she could make them—but what would Kate think? She gnawed on her pencil and went over the first one, once more.

> Some people are proud because of the
>   church they go to.
> Some people are proud because of the
>   clothes they wear.
> Some people brag about cars or money
>   or college

Or go around saying they've traveled
  everywhere.

You don't have a church or a car or a lot
  of money.
You haven't traveled around the world,
  it's true.
But you yourself are a person you can
  be proud of.
I'd rather be proud like you.

It sounded wrong, all at once. She thought
about Kate. Kate was not old enough to have a
car or travel or go to college. When she was,
though, she would still be the same Kate, Emily
decided. She could not imagine the other girl getting mixed-up about what was important. Still,
the poem sounded too much like grown-up talk.

She frowned at it, not knowing how to fix it.
Then she left it as it was.

As she flipped to the other one, her uncertainty vanished. This she had written from her
heart. She did not need to worry about whether
it was right or wrong. It was exactly what she
wanted to say. She read it over in a soft, soft
voice, just loud enough for herself to hear.

I used to wish that I could find
A friend, a special one.
I dreamed she would be wonderful.
I dreamed she would be fun.

I thought of us with jokes to tell
And secrets we would share.
I knew that when I hurt inside
She would really care.

I dreamed that we would laugh a lot
And hardly ever fight,
But if we did, then both of us
Would try to make it right.

I used to know a lot of girls
But never could I find
This one girl I kept wishing for,
The friend inside my mind.

Then you came banging in my life
And all I wished came true.
I have the friend I dreamed about—
You.

Coming to the end, Emily thought of Lindsay. Although Lindsay was through with chicken pox, Mrs. Ross would not let her come over to the Blairs' until the holidays were over. Laurel was due home, however, and other relatives had already come. Lindsay, when she phoned, complained about not seeing them, but she was clearly busy. Still, when Christmas and chicken pox were done with, Lindsay would be back with them again. Emily was glad. She, Lindsay, and Kate belonged together.

But it's queer, she thought now. I couldn't write this to Lin. For her I'd do a funny one.

"Emily . . ."

Emily thrust the poems under her pillow and leaned against it.

"Yes," she answered, her voice unnaturally bright.

Kate came in and perched on the edge of the bed.

"I have a suggestion to make," she said.

"A suggestion?" Emily was taken aback. Kate sounded so formal.

"The kids have run out of things to do," explained Kate, as though Emily had no idea of the state of things in the Blair house. "James and Jean are still in bed, of course, though James is getting pretty lively. But John is pacing around like a caged lion, and Ann keeps asking me how many HOURS till Christmas. I think we should do something to take their minds off waiting. We have two whole days to go."

"What kind of something?"

Kate bent down and straightened the top of her sock. Still leaning over, her face hidden, she answered.

"Um . . . I thought . . . maybe you should do that play you were talking about."

Emily could not believe her ears. Had Kate forgotten what kind of play it was? What part would she play?

Kate, sitting up, read Emily's mind as though it were a billboard.

"I won't be King Herod." She met her friend's startled gaze squarely, now that the worst was behind her. "I *could* be Mary, you know. She was Jewish."

"But you're not really . . . not that it matters!" Emily stammered lamely. "I mean . . ."

"Yeah, I know what you mean," Kate said. "Like Lindsay said, I'm nothing. Only I don't feel like nothing. I feel like me. I, my own self, don't want to be in the play. Not even to be Mary."

"How about Joseph?" Emily tried feebly, trying to break the tension.

"How about stage manager, director, wardrobe mistress, prompter, producer, set designer, and author's help?" Kate snapped back. She had come prepared. "They're always telling us at school that those people are as important as the actors."

"A family Christmas play," said Emily slowly.

It was coming back to her now—the special star, the small stable, the long road filled with travelers.

"We could put it on Christmas Day," she planned, caught up in it again. "But how could we keep it a secret?"

Kate had none of the author's doubts.

"We'll manage. All you have to do is write it," she said, "and help with a couple of other details."

After an hour of frenzied planning, the two of them went down and told Mrs. Blair no adults were to come to the third floor, no matter what. Then Emily took all her mother's shelf paper. They taped it, in long strips, to the wall of the big room Dad still talked of equipping with a Ping-Pong table. They gathered pencils, paint, brushes, and paint rags. Ann, overjoyed to be included, stirred jar after jar of paint with devoted care. Emily, Kate, and John conferred on what should be pictured, and they sketched in their ideas.

After lunch, while the little girls napped and James kept bouncing out of bed to check on their progress, the three of them started painting their scenery.

It showed the inside of a stable—a cow looking over her stall, a dove ("Looks more like a fat duck," James told them), a dog with spots, a cat like Willie which John drew ("Looks like a striped pig," James said), and a small window with a star shining in.

Emily had trouble with that star. However she tried to get its five points evenly distributed, it looked lopsided and off-center. Kate paused, her own paintbrush in midair, to watch. Emily painted over the star for the third time and sighed. This one thing had to be perfect. After all, it was her own star, shining brightly down on her through her own window, that had been the beginning of it all.

"Send John down here. I need him," Mother called. John went to see what she wanted.

"You know what, Emily?" Kate said suddenly. "You should make it a Jewish star."

"A Jewish star!"

"Wait. I'll show you." Kate put down her brush and went off to the room they shared. Emily heard the lid of her suitcase open. Then the other girl was back, a book in her hand. It was called *What Is a Jew?* and it had a star on the front, a complicated star made of interlocking triangles.

"It has six points." Kate showed her.

"But would it be all right to . . . ?" Emily stalled.

"Listen," Kate said, flipping through the pages. "I read it just the other day. Here."

The Shield of David, or Mogen David, is a six-pointed star made up of two triangles pointing in opposite directions. The star has no ancient Jewish origin or religious meaning.

She skipped the rest and closed the book. "So go ahead. Use it."

"But the triangles—"

"Oh, not the triangles. Just give it six points. It'll be easier."

Emily could see that. She sighed thankfully and began. Kate smiled as the other girl carefully painted a new star in the sky over Bethlehem.

"It does look better, doesn't it?" Emily eyed it uncertainly. The edges still wobbled.

"It's fine. Perfect. Now come and help do this wall."

Emily, dipping her brush in brown paint, glanced sideways at the book Kate had left on a nearby chair.

"When did you get that?" she asked, trying to sound offhand and sounding shy instead.

"I got it downtown. Not even at our store," Kate grinned. "I just thought maybe I'd learn something—but the man who wrote it says right in the introduction that he can't definitely, positively tell what a Jew is. And he's a rabbi!"

"Really?" Emily said, finding this beyond her. She was down on her knees, painting the bottom of the wall. Without stopping to think, she looked up and said, "You know what . . . I'm glad you didn't tell us you were part Jewish back when I first met you. I'm glad I liked you, just as you were, before you said—"

Something forbidding in Kate's face stopped her.

"I knew you were Christians the first night I was here for supper," Kate said. "I knew when your father asked the blessing. But it didn't make any difference to me."

Emily sat very still. She could have bitten her tongue off. If only John would come back. No, it was up to her. She must say something.

Kate spoke first. There was still a raw edge to her voice, but the coldness was gone.

"Emily, if we stay friends—and I'm Jewish and you're Christian—this is going to happen to us lots of times. We won't mean anything bad—"

"I didn't." Emily gulped. "I'm sorry. I just meant—"

"No, wait," Kate told her. "Let me think a minute."

They were silent while she put her thoughts in order. Then, beginning to paint again with great sweeps of her brush, she went on.

"We mustn't have to be careful. If we say the wrong thing, we must just forget it. Maybe we'll learn. But we mustn't be watching out all the time. We might end up talking about things like the weather. Safe things. I knew what you meant. Right when you said it, I knew. You're glad you didn't know I was different before you found out I wasn't. That doesn't sound like sense, does it?" she ended, with a spurt of laughter.

"What's not sense?" John asked, returning.

"Never mind," Kate said. She added maddeningly, "You're too young to understand. Emily understands me, don't you, Emily?"

"Yes," Emily said. "More or less."

She looked ahead, in a moment of vision, and saw the two of them, grown up, still friends, still different, still talking about real things and not minding hurts because they had so much that was good.

We're looking through each other's windows, she thought suddenly and smiled.

"Hey!" John cried. "It's finished."

They moved back to get the full effect. It was messy here and there. The animals did not look exactly the way they should. In fact they all could see what James had meant. But even James, who came out to look too, was impressed. It was so big, for one thing—and if you squinched up your eyes and used your imagination, you stood in a barn at night.

"Emily, you haven't written a word," Kate protested as Emily went bounding away in search of a manger.

"I'm thinking about it every minute," Emily called back.

She found an orange crate and some packing which looked reasonably like hay. Jean loaned Henriette to play the part of the Baby Jesus. Emily, struck by yet another inspiration, got the floodlight her father had bought to light up their evergreens out front.

"We need it, and I can't explain," she told her mother.

"Be it on your own head," her mother said calmly and went on vacuuming.

Finally Emily had to face up to the writing of the play.

"I'll leave you alone to think," Kate said quietly. "You know, even if it hadn't been the Christmas story, we couldn't have written it together. We don't write the same way. I have something else I have to do anyway."

Emily sat on her bed and stared into space.

Christmas words went back and forth in her mind.

Star . . . shepherds . . . lambs . . . no room in the inn . . .

None of them would come together and make sense. None of them held the beauty which had been there on the first night.

At last, in desperation, she got out the Bible. She was curled up, reading over the old, old words, when Kate came tiptoeing in to check on her progress.

"I don't have to write it," Emily told her, her voice hushed. "We can just use the words in here and act them out. Listen."

Kate sat beside her and Emily read aloud.

And there were in the same country shepherds abiding in the field . . .

It was Emily's decision, not Kate's, but Kate knew what Emily meant. The old words were beautiful, whether or not they were true.

"It's kind of like a poem, isn't it?" Kate said, wondering if it were all right to speak of it that way.

Emily nodded. "It's like a fairy tale too," she said, seeing it herself as she spoke. "The poor prince, and then the kings coming and the angels and shepherds. I love it."

She looked uncertainly at Kate. Kate had nothing to say, but she smiled reassuringly.

They spent the next day casting and collecting

costumes from here, there, and everywhere. Sophie agreed to play King Herod when they promised not to give her any lines.

Then the mail came and there was a letter for Kate.

"Oh," was all she said when Dad put it in her hand.

But as she read her mother's words, her face shone.

"Marilyn's better now they're there," she reported. "Nicky does have a hole in his heart, but Mother says lots of babies have them and are all right later on. She says she misses me . . ."

She read the signature to herself and tucked the letter into the hip pocket of her jeans. Throughout the long, busy day, Emily often saw her reach back and simply touch the folded letter, making sure it was really there.

The stockings were hung. The little children were bundled off to bed. Then it was Emily's and Kate's turn. They were half-asleep when bare feet pattered outside their bedroom door. Emily propped herself up on one elbow.

"Who is it?" she called softly.

"James," said an excited whisper. "Emily, is it morning?"

"Go back to bed," Emily told him. "It's only beginning to be night. I'll call you when it's morning, I promise. May visions of sugarplums dance in your head!"

James ran back to his room.

"I'm glad I'm here, Emily," Kate said then, all at once, her voice husky.

"I'm glad too," Emily told her. "I have a feeling in my bones that this is going to be the best Christmas of my entire life."

22

Christmas Begins

Emily wakened first. It was dark outside, but she knew, with a singing of her heart, that it was morning, that new snow had fallen while she slept, that Kate was asleep near her, and that it was Christmas. She lay perfectly still for one long moment, not wanting to let go of the wonder of it.

"Kate, Kate," she called then, bounding up, "Merry Christmas!"

Kate turned over sleepily and peered at her without recognition. Then the wonder came into her eyes too.

"Merry Christmas, Emily," she said.

Nobody was allowed to go down to the living room until the entire family was collected.

Strangest of all was having to wait for Mrs. Thurstone. Dad had brought her over the night before, after persuading her that Christmas morning, first thing, was something she must not miss. At last, they were ready. All eleven of them, in their robes, trooped down the stairs and in to the tree. Wilhelmina Shakespeare declined to stay, but Inky settled cosily on Kate's knee. Having Inky there gave her a feeling of belonging. He was hers, and so this room and these people were hers too.

Dad read aloud the story of the first Christmas. When he had finished, he said quietly, "Let's pray together."

The four small children folded their hands and bowed their heads. Emily simply sat still, her eyes open, watching the tall tree with the rainbow lights, seeing the top of Ann's bent head, waiting for what her father would say. She turned, on impulse, and looked at Kate beside her.

Kate was wishing she were anywhere else in the world. What should she do while these people prayed? Then she caught Emily's blue eyes, smiling quietly. Emily was not doing anything special. She was just waiting. Kate waited too.

"Dear Father, help each of us to find the important things in life and love them. Amen," Peter Blair said.

Was that all? Kate, braced for something quite different, laughed at herself. If everything today were that simple . . .

At last, the presents! So many, such wonderful presents! Emily opened a puppet John had made for her, a new dress from her parents, *Harriet the Spy* from Mr. Bloomfield and *The Long Secret* from Kate's mother, a hand mirror from Sophie, a five-cent package of Kleenex tissues and some Lifesavers from James. He had given everyone the same presents.

"Two each," he boasted happily, basking in their laughter.

"Here." Dad handed Kate and Emily identical boxes.

"'With affection from your neighbor, Anne Thurstone,'" Emily puzzled out the crabbed writing. She undid the wrapping carefully. Both of them had been given lockets which had been Mrs. Thurstone's when she was a girl.

"Time they belonged to young things again," she barked.

Emily's had butterfly wings inside it. It shimmered and changed color when she moved it. She thought she had never seen anything more beautiful. She struggled to thank the old lady.

"What a tarradiddle, to be sure!" Mrs. Thurstone said.

But Emily knew she was pleased.

Then she stopped thinking about her presents. Dad was reaching back under the tree where she had put the book of poems for Kate. He had it! He came across the room to them. But he was holding two packages again.

"'For Emily, with love, from Kate,'" Emily read, while Kate pronounced, "'For Kate, with love, from Emily.'"

They had had exactly the same idea. Emily had called her book *It's a Wonderful World*. It was covered in silver paper and had "by Emily Blair" on the front in fancy lettering. Kate's had a plain green cover and said simply *Poems* and underneath "by Kate."

"How did you ever guess, Miss Bloomfield?" Emily gushed, hiding her heart behind nonsense.

"Just exactly what I needed!" Kate returned.

Their eyes shone. They put the books down, unable to look in front of everybody.

"Time to clean up in here and have some breakfast," Mother said briskly before anyone could pry. "Come on, James."

Wrapping paper was picked up. They ate. They got dressed. Uncle Roger went to church. The others scattered through the big house, talking, putting gifts away, trying new toys, basting the turkey.

Emily and Kate sat down separately with the books they had made for each other. Kate, too, had written new poems. There was one very long one.

> In my family, we don't talk much about
>   loving.
> My mother never bakes us pies or knits
>   us socks.

More than once, she's put cream in my
    father's coffee—although he takes it
    black.
When she gets home from work, she
    collapses with her feet up.
I have to shake her awake when it's time
    to eat.
My father doesn't send her roses or
    valentines.
He just says "April, listen to this. April!"
Then she yawns and lights a cigarette
    and listens
While he reads her something by a man
    called Kafka.
Nobody asks me whether I've any
    homework
And I do not wait to be told to go to bed.
I used to think they didn't know I was
    there.
But they do. My father looks up, all at
    once,
And he says to me, "Katharine, tell me . . .
    what is truth?"
My mother leaves me to get the supper
    on—
But she brings me home twelve, brand
    new 2B pencils.
. . . Someday, I'll send my mother one
    dozen roses.
Someday, I'll knit my father a pair of
    socks.

> When I have children, I'll tell them, "It's
>   time for bed."
> But I'll also ask them, sometimes, "What
>   is truth?"
> And I'll leave them to get the supper—
>   and give them pencils.
> Loving isn't as simple as I once thought.
> And talking about it isn't what matters
>   most.

Emily went back to the beginning and read it again. So this was what Kate's mother and father were really like. She thought of her own parents. They were not like the Bloomfields. Yet, Emily, too, knew that loving was not simple.

She turned the page, knowing she would go back to this poem.

She's written a rhyming one, she thought in surprise. Kate's poems hardly ever rhymed.

She began to read quickly. At the end of the second line, she halted and started again, hearing what every word said to her.

> Sometimes in bed at night, I feel like the
>   only
> Person alive in the world—and I get
>   lonely.
> Then I say softly, "Emily
> is friends with me."

You're not the only one that counts. I
    have other names . . .
Your mother, my mother, Inky—and
    even James!
But the first, best thing I do
Is remember you.

Emily's eyes stung with tears. She looked up
and, through them, saw Kate standing in the
doorway.

"I read your poems," Kate said.

Emily swallowed.

"I read yours," she said.

"Are you guys playing a game or something?"
James asked, poking his head around Kate and
looking from one to the other.

"No," Emily told him. "We just don't know
what to say to each other."

"You must be sick!" he jeered.

Laughter untied their tongues. They told each
other and told each other how much they loved
the poems. Then Emily could not stay still a
moment longer. Without explaining, she jumped
up and ran away from the others, down the
stairs. Kate came pounding after her.

"Just in time to set the table," Mother said as
they dashed into the kitchen, "and you can mix
the cranberry punch, and . . . I have a million
jobs for both of you."

"Mother, it's Christmas!" Emily objected, with
no hope of reprieve.

"Yes, isn't it just," Mother said, closing the oven door. "While you're at it, see the beds are made. Sophie and I have not a finger to spare. Kate, I'm so glad you're here to help."

Emily yelled in outrage, but Kate only grinned.

"So'm I," she said happily. "Come on, Emily."

"Kate Bloomfield, have you gone mad?" Emily questioned.

"Don't worry about it, Emily," Mother said. "It's only 'Good will to men.' It'll pass in no time and she'll be as normal as you and I. Now, please, get busy."

"Wouldn't you like us to look after the children, too, while we're at it?" Emily asked too sweetly.

"A magnificent idea!" Mother assured her. "You see, Kate, how contagious brotherly love can be?"

Emily grabbed her friend's elbow and propelled her out of the kitchen before another disaster could overtake them.

"Never, never trust a parent!" she muttered darkly.

"I won't," Kate promised.

But she was giggling as she said it.

23

Emily's Play

E mily wished Christmas dinner would hurry up and be over. The play came next. Her stomach turned a somersault. She could not eat dessert.

"All right, GO!" Mother said at last. (Only James was plowing happily through a second piece of pie.) "Leave the rest, Kate. You can have something later. We'll be upstairs in half an hour."

The six children crowded out of the dining room, James grabbing a last-minute handful of nuts to keep himself from starving.

At the deserted table, the adults sipped their coffee.

"Listen." Uncle Roger spoke for them all. "It's quiet."

But there was no quiet on the third floor. Emily hurled orders right and left. Kate put people into costumes. Sophie wailed that she did not know what she was supposed to do.

"You're having stage fright," Emily told her. "It'll pass."

Crash! John and James overturned the manger. Jean flew to Henriette's rescue with a shriek. Kate, whirling to look, upset a box of straight pins.

"I want to be a wise man instead of a shepherd," Ann informed Emily gently.

Then it was time.

"Kate will help you, Sophie, I promise." Emily gripped Sophie with an iron hand to keep her from bolting.

Thank goodness for Kate! The teachers at school had been right about the supreme importance of stage managers, wardrobe mistresses, and prompters. Already Kate had her hands full, and the play had not begun.

The audience took their places. Emily, her knees knocking, stepped out in front of them. She blinked as Kate switched on the floodlight.

"This is a pageant," she said shakily. "It is called 'Under a Special Star.' Scene One takes place on the hills near Bethlehem."

A folding screen of Mother's hid the stable scenery at the beginning. Sophie and Ann, in bright-red bathrobes, were shepherds, with Inky as their sole sheep. (Willie had refused to cooperate.) The kitten did not seem to have grasped his part. He purred and licked Ann's chin.

"Nice sheep," Ann said, making sure the audience, at least, understood.

Emily read the words from the Bible, but the Sutherland children put in bits of their own whenever they thought it would help.

John was the whole heavenly host. He arrived in an excited rush, stumbling over the sheet he wore.

"Hurry down to Bethlehem," he commanded.

"Why?" Ann asked. "Is the Baby Jesus there?"

"I'm supposed to tell YOU that, Ann," John said in a loud whisper. "You don't know it yet."

"I do too!" Ann bristled with indignation.

John remembered his angelic role.

"The Baby Jesus is there!" he announced. "Hurry down and find him. Glory! Hallelujah!"

The "angels" departed into heaven. The shepherds did not move. Kate reached out a long arm and pulled Sophie off stage. Ann trotted after her, Inky still in her arms.

Emily and Kate shifted the screen. Jean, draped in a blue beach towel, was kneeling behind the manger.

"There, there, Jesus," she crooned to Henriette. "Go to sleep now."

John, now in Kate's brown poncho, suddenly became Joseph.

"Here come some shepherds, wife," he panted,

arriving at Jean's side in the nick of time.

Ann knelt by the manger. Sophie stood as though she were carved out of stone. Inky wriggled free and pounced off to play in the shadows.

Kate reclaimed Sophie and turned her into Herod with a cardboard crown.

James was all three wise men. Sophie stared over his head, her eyes glazed with fright.

Maybe Herod really looked like that, Emily thought, and read on.

"Here come three more strangers," Joseph said to Mary.

James, carrying the old poem box, entered grandly. He threw himself down before the manger and bowed so low his crown fell off. He plunked down the gift, scrambled up, and marched off grinning, crown in hand. Kate replaced it firmly.

"Don't bow so hard," she hissed.

Back he came, bearing a tall jar of Mother's. The third time, he arrived with a squat brass vase.

"This one's the gold," he explained.

He knelt beside Ann, and Emily began to sing softly.

Away in a manger,
No crib for a bed . . .

The little children joined in. Jean, wise in the ways of mothers, lifted Henriette out of the manger and rocked her gently in her arms as she sang.

It was over. The actors lined up and bowed. Emily pulled Kate out to stand with them, and they bowed again. The applause was magnificent.

Embarrassed, the boys began to clown.

"Hello, foolish man," jeered John, poking his brother.

"Let's see your wings!" James shouted, doubling over at his own wit. "Let's see your harp!"

Mother stood up. Trumpeting through cupped hands, she announced, "Cast party downstairs in five minutes. Leave all costumes up here, if you please." In her ordinary voice, she added, "All right, boys. Enough of that nonsense."

"Surely they aren't going to EAT?" Dad groaned.

"They didn't have dessert," Mother reminded him. "We didn't all indulge like you and Roger."

"I like a man who doesn't pick at his food," Mrs. Thurstone thrust in unexpectedly. "Give me a hand up, young man."

"Anything you say, gracious lady," Dad cried, rising to do her bidding.

Elizabeth Blair turned away from them and looked for the girls.

"Emily—and Kate, too—that was really lovely," she said.

Emily heard the words of praise, and she was glad her mother liked what they had done. But, all at once, she was too tired to answer. Her play was finished. In spite of the mistakes, she knew it had gone well—but it was done. She felt far away from everyone. Loss swept through her. Was she going to cry . . . or simply stand there, with nothing to say, forever? She did not know. If only she were in her own bed in her own room with the light out! Here there were so many people, so much noise . . . Moments ago she had been in Bethlehem, abiding in the fields, under a special star.

Kate glanced at her. Then she answered politely for both of them.

"Thank you. We liked doing it. It was really Emily's play though."

The others had left the attic. Kate, Emily, and Emily's mother were by themselves for an instant, in an island of quiet. Emily took a deep, unsteady breath and turned to follow the rest. Then she halted. Kate was saying something. Still not caring, still not part of the world around her, Emily waited, listened.

"Mrs. Blair," Kate began. In her hurry to get the words out while she had the courage, she sounded almost rude. "My mother told me to say thank you today for having me here for Christmas. She said you were wonderfully kind, especially since it's Christmas. And I was to tell you so."

Mother interrupted or tried to. "Kate, there's no need—"

The girl ignored her. She went on doggedly, her sentences jostling each other.

"My mother's right, and I do thank you and all that . . . but I want to say something else. I . . ."

She paused, but this time Elizabeth Blair had enough insight to be quiet. "You said Christmas meant loving . . . well, it's not Christmas . . . I mean, I think it's just you . . . all the time. What I'm trying to say is, when you came to our place and talked to my mother that night . . . that was more than Christmas. My mother was so worried and you, you . . . and you kept Inky for me too . . . Oh, I don't know how to say it!" she finished, swallowing and looking as though she wished, with all her heart, she had not started to try.

Emily's mother reached out and drew the girl close. She kissed the hot cheek swiftly.

"You say it very well, Kate," she said, "and I thank you. But loving works two ways, you know."

Now she paused, wondering how much to say, whether or not to share with this perceptive child her own loneliness. Kate leaned against her, not making a sound. The woman found her next words slowly. They sounded as jumbled and full of feeling as Kate's own.

"Emily must have told you about our 'impossible summer.' Well, it was impossible for me. And even since school began, I have met few people here in Riverside. I don't suppose you've ever guessed what it meant to me talking with your mother. She has made my Christmas so. . . so much more joyous. . . lending me her daughter and . . . beginning to be my friend. Goodness, Kate, you've made me cry!"

Kate, in tears herself, hid her face in Mrs. Blair's shoulder.

"Here," Emily said brusquely.

Taking the package of tissues James had given her from her pocket, she handed each of them a piece. She had to use one herself. All three of them blew their noses long and loud.

"Elizabeth, where's this party?" Dad shouted up the stairs.

"Oh, just once, I'd like to be able . . . Do I look all right?" Mother asked the girls. They nodded.

"Coming!" she called back.

"Race you down, Kate Bloomfield," Emily said, alive again and sounding like James.

"You're on," Kate shot back.

But Emily had a head start.

24

The Important Things

Kate went home. School began. The Bloomfields had Emily and her parents to dinner.

"He makes me feel as though I haven't read a book in ten years," Peter Blair complained when they got home.

"Well, have you?" teased his wife. Then she added, "Anyway, he doesn't. You're just being silly. It's easier to understand now why Kate's the girl she is, though."

"What did you and April talk about when we got off on inflation?" he asked.

"Our daughters," Mother said, with a smile at Emily. "What else?"

January brought really cold weather. The big

house was drafty, and the Blairs used their fireplaces. James knocked out a front tooth playing hockey. Inky turned from a kitten into a small cat. Kate and Emily stayed overnight at Lindsay's and the three of them tried pulling taffy. They got it all over everything.

"Never again!" vowed Mrs. Ross. She looked darkly at Kate.

Yet, even though new days kept arriving full of expected and unexpected events, Emily Blair felt somehow that everything was finished. Finishing, anyway. About to end.

She knew, for one thing, that Aunt Deborah was getting better. Her parents and Uncle Roger sat up late, talking, planning. Emily wanted to ask, ached to know what was to happen. She said nothing at all.

At the next Quill Club meeting, Lindsay produced the first chapter of a novel. She called it *Felicity Finds Happiness*. Kate and Emily laughed so hard at it they almost rolled off Emily's bed. Lindsay shook her head at the pair of them.

"Go ahead, children, laugh! When it turns out to be a Best Seller, don't think I won't remember."

Kate snorted. "I'd rather be a Great Poet than a Best Seller any day," she informed Lindsay.

Emily looked from one to the other.

"I plan to be both," she told them.

James fell over the bannister from halfway up the stairs and did not even hurt himself. John, crossing his bedroom, tripped and cracked a bone in his foot. Daisy was lost again and found. Emily tried skis and spent most of her time sitting down. Kate, who now felt like a "real aunt," started to knit her nephew a sweater. Kate was no knitter. Sophie finally finished it for her. Mrs. Thurstone came over more and more often to supper.

Still, Emily knew that everything was about to change. Underneath the Emily who helped with the dishes and did her homework, who wrote a poem about new snow, who took Jean and Ann sledding, who began to wish for spring, who had long conversations with Wilhelmina Shakespeare, another Emily waited and watched, expecting each day to be the different one.

I'm not ready, she thought once.

But when she asked herself "Ready for what?" she did not know.

Valentine's Day came and went. Saint Patrick's Day was over. Easter displays were beginning to appear in store windows.

"It must seem queer not believing in Easter," Lindsay said to Kate.

Before Kate could think of answering, Emily's temper flared.

"What's so queer about it?" she demanded, rounding on a startled Lindsay. "Do you feel queer not believing in . . . in . . ."

She cast about wildly in her mind for something appropriate.

". . . in Ramadan?" she finished triumphantly.

"Emily, what ARE you talking about?" Lindsay wanted to know.

Emily took a deep breath, readying herself for a long, heated, and crystal-clear explanation which would put Lindsay in her place and save Kate embarrassment. She only wished she was a little more certain of what Ramadan really was.

Kate stopped her before she started.

"Calm down, Emily," she said, her voice cool and not particularly grateful. "Ramadan has nothing to do with it. It's that month or whatever when the Mohammedans fast," she told Lindsay. Lindsay nodded, remembering. They had all learned about it in school. "Lin doesn't feel queer about Ramadan because nobody around her does anything about it," Kate went on, this time to Emily. "Easter's everywhere I go. But it doesn't bother me, so let's forget it."

"Okay," Lindsay said agreeably.

Emily had shrunk into herself. She did not speak. As the three of them walked on in silence, Kate wondered what Emily was thinking.

Maybe she won't ever talk about things like that again, Kate worried.

Then she remembered the poem Emily had given her. She knew it by heart.

> I dreamed that we would laugh a lot
> And hardly ever fight,
> But if we did, then both of us
> Would try to make it right.

She was comforted. Still, she did hope Emily had learned not to defend her when she did not need defending.

If it comes to fighting, Kate thought with a private grin, I'm a better fighter than Emily any day of the week.

She knew the hurt was forgotten one afternoon when the two of them were alone, and Emily said dreamily, "Kate, do you believe in God?"

Kate's guard went up, in spite of herself. She answered stiffly.

"Do you mean me myself or Jewish people?"

Emily, sprawled on the couch, sat up and stared at her.

"For crying out loud, I KNOW what Jewish people believe," she snapped.

She lay back suddenly, laughing. When she did not explain, Kate, her voice still sharp, questioned, "What's so funny?"

Emily wished, for a moment, she had not started this, but it was too late to back down. Besides, she and Kate had decided, long ago, to be truthful with each other.

"It's just my dopey mother. Ages ago I asked her if Jews believed in God, and she said . . ."

"What?" prodded Kate.

Emily blushed faintly, but her eyes were dancing.

"She said '*Believe* in Him? They *invented* Him!'"

She darted a look at Kate. Kate was grinning.

"Then she got really mad at me." Emily settled back comfortably and went on to remember the rest of it. "She said she wondered why they'd bothered carting me to Sunday school. Hadn't I ever heard of Moses and Abraham? Then guess what she said?"

"What," Kate said again, but easily this time.

"She told me to remember that Jesus had never heard of a difference between Jews and Christians and that he was celebrating the Passover on the night he was arrested. She said he was a lot more Jewish than you are."

They were both silent, pondering this.

"I never thought of it like that," Kate said at last.

"Neither did I." Emily turned over onto her stomach and looked at Kate. "But I was asking you about God. Do you believe in Him or not?"

"I try not to think about it mostly," Kate confessed. "I don't really believe, I guess. But I don't exactly *not* believe either. Mostly I think about something else."

Emily was astonished.

"I like thinking about Him," she said. "Only I keep changing my mind. Sometimes He's Someone I know, as real as my parents—only a spirit, of course. Then, the next minute, I start wondering if maybe the whole thing's made up. My mother says that you have to 'grow up to God.'"

"Maybe." Kate was not prepared to commit

herself. She grinned suddenly. "I guess I'm still a mere child, Emily."

"I wouldn't be surprised," Emily conceded, and the discussion ended in shared laughter.

Then, one night late in March, the change Emily had been half-expecting and half-dreading ever since Christmas arrived. When she looked back on it, that night was like the afternoon, months before, when she had discovered the apartment locked against her. This time she did not find her mother out. Her mother came up to find her in bed.

She was almost asleep when the light knock on her door roused her. Not waiting to be invited, Elizabeth Blair entered the small room under the eaves.

"Don't," Mother said quietly as Emily reached for the lamp switch. "I can see perfectly in all this moonlight. May I sit down?"

"Sure," Emily said, moving over to make room on the bed.

Her voice felt tight in her throat. Her fists balled up under the covers. What was it? Why had her mother come?

"Deborah is almost well again," Elizabeth Blair said.

She sounded deeply happy. Yet there was a wistfulness in her voice, as though she, like Emily, did not feel ready. "The doctors say she can come home at the end of April."

"That's good," Emily managed.

"Of course, the Sutherlands will want their own place then," Mother went on steadily. "We thought of keeping this house and having it divided into apartments so we could all live here . . ."

Emily's heart leapt with hope.

". . . but it isn't practical," Mrs. Blair said. "Your father is putting it on the market in June."

"You mean . . . he's going to sell it?"

Emily wondered if that was really her voice speaking. It cracked queerly, and it sounded cold and distant.

"Yes, Emily, I'm afraid so. If anyone had told me a few months ago that I'd be sorry to see the last of this place . . . I'd . . . well, I'd have laughed. But things have changed so over this year. And I do know how much you love it. Right from the first day. Remember all those windows you washed?"

Mother laughed, but Emily could not bring herself to do more than move her head in assent on the pillow.

"We will be here a while longer," her mother went on, as though the girl had spoken. "Aunt Deborah will come here at first. And we'll stay here together till summer. Then we'll move to a place of our own."

"An apartment?"

"No. But a small house—without four guest rooms."

But the kids, Emily thought wildly. And Kate.

What would her life be like without John and James, Jean and Ann? They were part of her every day now. They belonged where she did.

She swallowed hard, but the lump in her throat did not move.

"Emily, we'll all still be here in Riverside," her mother said. She reached out. Pulling one of Emily's hands from under the covers, she held it tightly in hers.

"What about Sophie . . . and Wilhelmina Shakespeare?"

"Sophie will go with Deborah at first, and Willie will go with Sophie . . . but we'll keep Inky for Kate. And Sophie will come back to us. I'm going to be needing Sophie myself in August."

"In August," Emily repeated dully.

August was worlds and years away. She would not have her own special room any more in August. She would not have her star. She would not even have her window. She would not have the children, or Sophie, or Willie. She would not have . . .

"Emily . . . Emily, are you listening to me?"

"Yes," Emily said, rousing and hearing her mother again.

"I'm going to have a baby," Mrs. Blair said. Emily did not believe her ears.

"You're going to—" she started.

"Yes . . . have a baby . . . in August. We thought one child would do, but we've . . . we thought we could do with a baby. Emily, are you pleased?"

Emily sat up suddenly, gripping her mother's hand.

Why, her world was not ending! Or maybe it was—but a new one was opening before her. A baby!

Elizabeth Blair felt, in that moment, that she, not Emily, was the child. She waited for approval or shock. Even tears! When her daughter sat there, bolt upright in the darkness, not saying a word, she thought, She needs time.

She smiled wryly, for she herself had needed time. She had known for months—yet she was still trying to believe it would really happen. There must be another way to reach Emily though . . . something steadying a mother could say, something that would begin to put her daughter's world back together.

"You'll still have Kate," she said into the silence. "I know you love this room, Emily, but things must change sometimes. I do so want you to be happy."

Emily looked up. Her star was there. It was hard to find because of the bright tide of moonlight, but she could see it, framed in her window, and she would always be able to find it. She remembered the night when Sophie came, and she and Jean and Ann had slept out in the tent. She had thought her star was lost that night. But she had looked again and found it. She just had to look from a different place. It had never left her.

And there are other stars, she thought. Other stars and other windows.

In that moment, deep inside herself, she felt the steadfastness of important things.

"Mother," she said eagerly, "suppose the baby turns out to be a boy like James."

"Oh, Emily," Mother said. "Oh, Emily."

"I'd like that," Emily said.

About the Author

Jean Little has published numerous popular and award-winning picture books and young adult fiction titles, including *From Anna*, *Hey World Here I Am!*, *Revenge of the Small Small* and *Mine for Keeps*. She was born in Taiwan and grew up in Ontario, receiving her degree in English and literature from the University of Toronto. She now lives near Elora, Ontario in an old stone farmhouse with her sister and four-year-old great niece, four dogs and two cats. She does her writing with a talking computer and travels extensively with her seeing eye dog, Ritz.